Changing
of the Guard

Changing
of the Guard

by Karen Thomas

1 8 🖋 1 7

——— HARPER & ROW, PUBLISHERS ———

Cambridge, Philadelphia, San Francisco, London, Mexico City, São Paolo, Singapore, Sydney

——— NEW YORK ———

Changing of the Guard
Copyright © 1986 by Karen Thomas
Designed by Joyce Hopkins
1 2 3 4 5 6 7 8 9 10
First Edition

Library of Congress Cataloging-in-Publication Data
Thomas, Karen.
    Changing of the guard.

    Summary: After the death of her beloved grandfather,
sixteen-year-old Caroline resists change, spending her
time with an elderly grandmother or alone, until a
flamboyant new girl at school draws her reluctantly
into a friendship.
    [1. Friendship—Fiction.   2. Grandparents—Fiction.
3. Death—Fiction.   4. High schools—Fiction.
5. Schools—Fiction]   I. Title.
PZ7.T36697Ch 1986   [Fic]   85-45249
ISBN 0-06-026163-3
ISBN 0-06-026164-1 (lib. bdg.)

Changing
of the Guard

1

I sat erect in my seat, resisting the sway of the dingy yellow school bus as it rattled and creaked down Rural Route One. It was a little game I played with myself—to anticipate each jolt and steel myself against it.

The roar of the bus was so deafening I had to press back in my seat and cock my head in order to hear the conversation between the two girls sitting behind me. I knew who they were—Jill Watson and Marybeth Lorch. But I doubted if they knew who I was.

Jill was speaking. ". . . so Mr. Bauman goes, 'If $2x$ equals 44, then x would equal 22. Do you think you understand it now?' And she goes, 'Well, I guess. Except I still don't see where you get the *x*.' Can you believe her? She is so stupid! I don't know why she signed up for algebra."

"She probably thinks she's cute or something," Marybeth offered. "Maybe she just wanted Mr. Bauman's attention." Both girls giggled and leaned into each other as if they were sharing a private joke.

The front wheels of the bus hit a rut, and I braced myself as it jerked to a stop. This was where I got off. The corner of Rural Route One and Whitneyville Road. The motions of the bus were so familiar to me, I could pinpoint our exact location at any given moment with my eyes shut. I gathered my books and papers from the seat beside me and made my way to the front of the bus, all the while staring down at the label on my notebook.

Caroline Warner
Grade 10
Phone 372–0561

My phone number is a constant source of irritation to me. If the seven had only been a four, the number would have contained all the digits from zero to six. My home address is much better—2358 Whitneyville Road. Two plus three equals five, three plus five equals eight. Numbers have always intrigued me, and they've always been easy for me to remember—either because they grated at my nerves or because they fell together so pleasingly.

"See you on Monday." The bus driver nodded. The door groaned as she pulled the lever.

"Thank you," I murmured, stepping off the bus. I was the only one to get off at the stop. The rest of the kids on the bus lived a little farther down the road in the subdivision.

I waited, motionless, until the bus had disappeared in a cloud of dust. My feet were begging for their freedom. I pulled off my shoes and socks and dug my toes deep into the sun-drenched earth. Using my foot, I righted a sign that was lying facedown in the dirt. "Clean Fill Wanted."

I studied the sign and sadly traced along the letters with my toes. A wisp of hair had managed to free itself from my barrette. I wet two fingers and brushed it back to the nape of my neck, then turned and started down Whitneyville Road and home.

It was hot. The temperature hovered near eighty degrees and the day was perfectly still. It wasn't exactly typical for late September in Michigan, especially this far north. There'd been a brief cold snap in early September, but it had moved on and been replaced by a breathless, weighty heat. Indian summer. Most people are grateful for an extension of summer. I prefer the seasons to occur on schedule.

There was not the slightest trace of a breeze as I

3

walked along, yet every few moments the earth would cough up a spiraling ball of dust that would travel quickly forward as it dissipated over everything in its path. I squeezed my eyes shut as the cloud rolled soundlessly over me.

In the near distance saws buzzed and hammers hammered and the crew foreman barked orders to his men as yet another house was slapped together on what used to be the Warner Farm. I don't know how many houses had gone up. I stopped counting at twenty.

I caught a halting motion out of the corner of my eye and bent low to get a closer look. With a practiced hand I swooped up the toad. I held it firmly, my thumb pinning the ancient-looking creature on its back. When I blew on him, a puff of dust rose like steam and vanished away. I stroked his dry, knobby head.

"Things sure have changed around here, haven't they . . ." I whispered. The toad stopped struggling and lay motionless in my grasp. When I set him down, he waited a full ten seconds before springing to life and leaping away.

I wiped my hands on my jeans. To say things had changed around here was the understatement of the century.

Two years earlier—just a few months before he died—my Grandpa Warner sold all but three acres of his two-hundred-acre farm to a real-estate investor.

Grandma Warner still lives in the house on what little land is left.

Together my grandparents had worked the farm all their married lives. Grandma handled the household and the business end of things, and Grandpa did the growing. He grew peaches as big as grapefruit; crisp, sweet apples—MacIntosh, Delicious, Ida Reds, and Rome; Concord grapes; Bartlett pears; a few melons and tomatoes; and sweet, dark cherries the size of fifty-cent pieces. Grandpa's crops never failed.

There were a few minor losses over the years, but even when other farms in our area were devastated by January thaws that tricked the buds into thinking spring, or killer frosts in May, or no rain in July, Grandpa Warner's crops would come through nearly unscathed.

Every day Grandpa walked the orchards—with me, whenever possible, following behind. We'd walk in silence between the perfect rows of trees, Grandpa pausing now and again to touch a branch or pat a trunk and whisper a few words of advice or encouragement. "Don't be fooled," he'd tell the tender buds, "it's still the dead of winter." Or, to the tiny new fruits, "You hang in there, little ones. Rain is coming soon." Sometimes he'd simply tell the trees they were good or strong or lovely.

One spring a tornado blew in across Lake Michigan, and, while everyone else raced for shelter, Grandpa and I stood bold as can be in the middle of the orchard with our eyes closed and our arms folded across our chests. The tornado touched down and cut a swath through the farm to the north of us, picked up and jumped over our orchard, then roared through the farm on our south side. There was an aerial picture in the newspaper showing the tornado's path of destruction on either side of us. The caption underneath it read: "Tornado spares Warner orchard." But I knew who had really spared it.

My grandparents were nearly forty when Dad was born. Grandma Warner had had several miscarriages before that, so when Dad came along, she kind of went a little overboard caring for him. At least that's what Grandpa Warner always said. Dad was the first person in the history of his family to go to college. He grew up protected and gentle and too soft to work in the dirt. Nevertheless, Grandpa Warner adored him, and, when it was time to give up the farm, he did it without so much as a blink. I'm just glad Grandpa died before he saw what became of his orchards.

Mr. Humphrey, the investor, turned right around and sold the land at a tidy profit to Magnum International. Their computer division had moved into our town a few years before that and had quickly grown into a monster of a business. Our little town didn't have enough people to support the work being done there, so the company was forced to import workers from other cities and states.

That's when things really began to snowball. More people meant more of everything: places to shop, schools, a bowling alley and skating rink and movie theater, restaurants, Laundromats, and on and on and on. It also meant more houses had to be built, and that was the end of Warner Orchard. Magnum International cleared the land and turned it into a subdivision. Within weeks it was gone. The whole orchard. Gone.

The trees Grandpa had planted with his own hands and nurtured with his own life were ripped out in a moment. I stayed in my room the whole time with the windows closed and the shades drawn and a pillow over my head. I had learned the language of those trees and I was afraid I'd hear them scream.

The idea of ghosts appeals to me, the idea that the spirits of the dead live on, walking in the places they used to walk and guarding the people they used to love. Sometimes I have dreams about Grandpa, but I have never once felt his presence. There is no place left for him to be.

Well, they tore the sign down, too. The one that read: "Warner Orchard . . . Fruit in Season . . . U-Pick or Ready-Picked." They replaced it with a bigger sign with fake antiquing and fake gilded letters that read:

OLD ORCHARD ESTATES
COUNTRY LIVING AT ITS FINEST

What a laugh. The jerks who thought Old Orchard Estates was country living at its finest did not know one thing about living in the country.

The houses in the subdivision come in three styles: ranch, split-level, and two-story colonials. The exteriors have different kinds of brick and colors of aluminum siding to try to trick you into thinking each house is unique. But the REAL plus is that there is one whole tree for every three houses. I mean, how lucky can you get? Just think. Every third day your family could go out and sit under it! That's really getting back to nature.

Just outside our gate I was greeted by a clear and sweetly haunting melody as it drifted from the house. Dad was home.

The tune he played on his clarinet was so familiar I could hum it backward. If you were hearing him play it for the first time, you'd think he was improvising. And maybe that's the way it started out. But for someone like me who'd heard the same song all her life, the patterns were structured and defined and unmistakably his. Dad plays the clarinet unlike any other person on this earth. In fact, when I was four years old I heard the clarinet being played in a Veterans' Day Parade and didn't even realize it was the same instrument!

"I'm home, Dad," I called.

The music continued to the end of the measure, then stopped. "Hi, Caroline!" he answered. "You made it through another day, I see." He walked into the kitchen and blew me a kiss. I caught it and threw one back.

A batch of oatmeal cookies arranged in perfect rows was set out to cool on the kitchen counter.

"Um! You've been making cookies!" I picked one up. It was still warm and gooey enough to mold into my palm.

"Yeah," Dad said, "I have to do something to fill up my time."

Dad's the supervisor in charge of production at a factory that makes plastic parts for the trim on automobiles. The economy in Michigan was pretty bad for a while and hit the car industry especially hard. Dad's plant had to cut back to a three day workweek.

"How long are you going to have short weeks?" The raisins in my cookie were hot and burned against my front teeth. I sucked in some air to cool them. "I thought the economy was getting better."

"I don't know, Toots." Dad drew his bare foot around the grouting between the floor tiles. "The economy *is* better, so it's pretty hard to figure out. There are a lot of rumors around the shop." Dad reached over and took a small cookie. He put the whole thing in his mouth. "I'm not really certain what's going on," he said as he chewed. "Things are pretty strange."

"Are you scared, Dad?"

Dad took another cookie and tapped the crumbs off. "Oh, a little. But things are bound to change one way or the other real soon. And, in the meantime, we'll be okay with Mom working and all." He edged closer to me and squeezed my arm. "I don't want you to worry about it."

"No," I promised, as best I could. "I won't."

Dad winked at me, then steadied his gaze. "It'll all work out." He unscrewed the lid from the cookie jar and began placing the cookies inside, the cooler ones first.

"When's Mother going to be home?" My hands were sticky from the cookie, and I turned to rinse them in the sink.

"Not till around six. They're starting to get their Christmas shipments in, so she's pretty busy."

Mom works as a buyer at Klugg's, a large department store that recently opened in town.

I flicked the cool water from my hands and snapped a paper towel from the dispenser. "Christmas shipments in September?"

"Don't go getting your blood in a flood." Dad chuckled. "Stores have to prepare well in advance for their busy seasons. Are you going over to Grandma's?"

"Yeah, I was planning on it. Have you heard from her today?"

Dad screwed the lid back on the cookie jar and buffed out the smears his fingers had left on the glass with a dish towel. "I tried calling her several times, but she didn't answer. Of course, that doesn't mean much with her."

I smiled in agreement. "Well, I think I'll get going, then."

"Okay." Dad nodded. "Do you have any plans for the weekend?"

I stiffened. "No. Not really. I . . . I thought I'd just mess around. And I have to finish writing a poem for English."

Dad's mouth twisted into a slight grimace, but he didn't say anything. My parents are always on me to make some friends and get involved at school.

"You be home by six," he said, the resignation in his voice coming through loud and clear.

I glanced at the kitchen clock to make sure my watch was synchronized with it.

"I will," I promised. I wound my watch as tight as it would go.

2

Grandma's house is just a short distance away. I ran to the corner of Whitneyville Road and Rural Route One. To the right was Grandma's house, the subdivision to the left. I always promised myself I wouldn't look to the left when I reached the intersection, but I always did. Quickly, though.

The road is a lot wider now than it used to be. I imagine they'll be blacktopping it sometime soon, maybe even putting in sidewalks. Warners' road. My road.

Grandpa Warner taught me how to drive his pickup truck when I was only seven or eight years old. He'd let me sit on his lap when we'd drive into town for supplies or to make deliveries. As soon as I was tall enough to reach the pedals, he'd let me drive all by myself on the gravel road leading to town while he catnapped in the passenger seat. My parents would die if they knew, but it's a good thing Grandpa taught me.

The summer I was ten Grandpa and I had driven out to a far corner of the orchard to cut dead branches from the Red Haven peach trees. We'd been working all morning, Grandpa doing the pruning while I hauled the rotted wood to a compost heap. We were nearing the end of our chore and I'd just poured a cup of ice water when, suddenly, the blade on Grandpa's power saw snapped and cut off Grandpa's thumb. It flew toward me and landed with a soft thud at my feet.

Grandpa ripped his shirt off and wadded it around his hand. "Pick it up!" he shouted.

I stood there with my eyes open as wide as my mouth.

"Caroline!" he screamed. "Pick up my thumb!"

I bent and picked it up. The warmth was already leaving it.

"Now put it in your cup and get into the truck!" he commanded.

I plunked the thumb into my ice water.

Grandpa ran to the truck and jumped in. I moved more slowly for fear I'd drop the cup and have to touch his thumb again. Once in the driver's seat, I carefully passed the cup to him.

We roared through the orchard, spraying up dust and hitting every pothole along the way. By the time we reached the road, blood was dripping from Grandpa's makeshift bandage.

"Turn left," Grandpa Warner instructed. He was holding his wrapped hand over his head. His face was gray.

"But Grandpa!" I questioned. "I have to turn right to get you to a doctor!"

"I want you to drive me to Doc Schneider's."

"Doc Schneider is a veterinarian!" I protested.

"Are you going to let me bleed to death, or are you going to do as you are told!"

Grandpa had never spoken to me in that tone of voice before. I turned left.

Doc Schneider's place was a good three miles up the road, but we arrived there in less than two minutes. Grandpa jumped from the truck and ran into Doc Schneider's house without knocking. By the time I got there Doc and Grandpa were arguing.

"No, you ain't gonna call an ambulance," I heard Grandpa say. "You're going to sew it back on."

"It won't work, John," Doc said firmly. "You need to be in a hospital. Clinton Center is only twenty miles from here."

"A hospital!" Grandpa scoffed. "Once they get you

14

in there, they don't never let you out." Grandpa turned and walked to the closet where Doc kept his medical bag. He snatched it from the shelf and shook it at Doc. "My early crop'll be ready for harvest next week. Now. Are you going to do the sewing, or am I?" he demanded.

Doc was still seated at his desk, staring into the cup containing Grandpa's thumb. "I'll do it, John, but only as a temporary measure. You've got to promise me you'll go straight into Clinton when I'm through."

Grandpa didn't look at him. His jaw was set as rock hard as his mind.

Doc sighed. "Let's get you cleaned up."

Of course, Grandpa never did go into Clinton. Not then and not ever. And the thumb took hold! Within weeks it had healed inside and out. Grandpa had some stiffness and loss of function with it, but so little no one would really have noticed.

I asked him about it once. I asked him how he got his thumb to grow back. He looked at me oddly for a moment. "Couldn't spare it," he answered.

I keep the cup on my bookshelf at home. I was going to throw it away once. But I couldn't spare it.

Just as I started across the road a Magnum International truck roared by. I had to jump back out of the way. The driver blasted his airhorn at me. His license plate number was FQ 49J. No sense. No sense at all.

When the dust settled, Grandma's house came into view. It was a two-story house made of red brick. The main part was once perfectly square, but over time it had lost its posture and now leaned inward. A great white porch stretched across the front. Some of the windows had raggedy shutters clinging to them; others had shed them years ago, and the shutters lay on the ground where they had fallen.

As the years had passed, bushes and vines had sprouted and claimed the house as their own. They snaked up the porch and over the brick and even covered the windows. It was always dark and damp inside the house. It had become a part of the earth.

The familiar old house beckoned me and I raced toward it.

Old Bill whimpered when he spotted me. I took a detour from my path to the house and walked over to where he was chained.

"Hi, Fella. How ya doin'?" I brushed some of the dust from his coat and stroked his muzzle.

Old Bill clawed at his ear with his paw and panted, his soulful eyes avoiding mine.

"What's the matter, Poochie? You don't like being chained up, do you? . . ."

I scratched his ear where he'd had an itch. "It's not fair, is it?"

Old Bill flicked his tail and moaned.

Bill was sixteen years old, two months older than

I, and he had been allowed to roam free until just a few years ago. Right after Grandpa Warner died, Old Bill started running away every chance he got. He'd be gone for a day or two, come home to eat, then leave again. Nobody could figure out where he was until the day Grandma, Mom, Dad, and I went to visit Grandpa's grave. Well, there was Old Bill. He'd made a kind of nest for himself against the headstone out of one of Grandpa's old work shirts. There were several places around the grave site where small holes had been dug, and when we cleared the mounds of earth away, we found some of Old Bill's dog bones, along with Grandpa's watch and handkerchief and measuring tape.

We have no idea how Old Bill knew Grandpa was buried there, but when we found him pressed against the headstone we all stood there and cried. Nobody said a word.

For a while after that, we let Old Bill spend his days at the cemetery, but when the work crews swarmed in to clear the orchard, Old Bill completely lost his mind. He'd bark at the workmen and nip at their feet. He came home limping pretty badly one night, and Grandma decided it would be best for both Old Bill and the work crews if she kept him chained from then on.

I'm not so convinced it was the best thing for Bill. He'd dug holes all around the perimeter of his chain's

17

length in a vain attempt to free himself.

"You're a good, good doggie, Bill," I soothed him. "I'll take you for a walk tomorrow."

As I turned to walk toward the house, Old Bill made a high-pitched squeak and sighed. I didn't look back. Nothing but his freedom would ever make Old Bill happy again.

The screen door leading into Grandma's house groaned in protest when I pushed it.

"Grandma? Are you here?" I called.

There was no answer.

"Grandma? Gram? Where are you?" I stepped over two empty bushel baskets in the hall that led into the kitchen.

"You wipe your feet! I don't want nobody tracking dirt into my kitchen!"

I rubbed my bare feet briskly across the hand-tied rag rug at the entrance to the kitchen. "Hi, Grandma. It's me!" The frail, gray-haired woman seated at the table ignored me.

"Stop your hollering!" she snapped. "You think I'm deaf or something?"

I crossed over to my grandmother and kissed the top of her head. She was peeling apples, then slicing them into a large iron kettle at her feet. A couple dozen jars of applesauce were meticulously lined up on the kitchen shelf nearest the old gas stove.

"Looks like you've been busy," I remarked as I took in the scene.

"Oh, once in a while," Grandma replied, "especially when I bend over or get up too fast. But now is no time to talk about my dizzy spells, girl. You get over to that stove and give the sauce a good stir."

I glanced toward the stove. There was nothing on the burner. Mentioning the fact, I knew, would be futile. I walked to the stove, stood there a few minutes, then returned to the table.

"How's it coming?" Grandma asked without looking up from her chore.

"Fine," I assured her. "Just fine."

"Good." She smiled. "These are the last of the apples right here. Maybe enough for three, four more quarts. You think that'll get us through the winter?" There were several potatoes on the table. Grandma picked one up and peeled it. I remained silent until she began slicing it into the apple pot.

"Wait, Grandma. I . . . I think that's a potato. . . ."

Grandma looked up at me with her startlingly blue eyes, then stared at the white sphere in her hand. She brought it to her nose and sniffed sharply. "Why, you're right!" she exclaimed, laughing and shaking her head. "Imagine that! A potato in the applesauce. That'd be a fine howdy-do!"

Grandma laid her knife down and wiped her hands

19

on her apron just as the clock in the living room softly chimed five times. "My goodness!" she exclaimed. "Where has the day gone?"

The fact that there were some things Grandma could hear with no difficulty made me wonder if she was becoming deaf or simply more selective.

"Would you like me to make you some supper, Grandma?" I asked.

"Already had it," she said. "Been up since four-thirty this morning." The lines around her mouth briefly deepened with pride.

I walked over behind Grandma and massaged the back of her thin, wrinkled neck. "Why do you do that, Grandma? You shouldn't get up so early."

"Work's gotta be done, girl. Ain't nobody else going to do it if I don't." Grandma reached back and pulled the pins from the braid coiled loosely at the base of her neck. "Brush my hair like a good girl."

I undid the braid and got Grandma's brush from the top of the refrigerator where she kept it. Grandma's hair is long—nearly to her waist. And the grayer it gets, the coarser it becomes. The hairbrush is eighty-five years old. Just like Grandma. It had been a christening gift. The ivory handle is cracked and deep yellow, the bristles so soft they merely skim the surface of Grandma's hair.

Slowly, hypnotically, I began stroking the yellow-gray mass and was immediately caressed by its warm, sweet smell. Grandma sprays her hair every day with some kind of lilac mixture she makes herself. She stores the concoction in an ancient glass milk bottle, pouring it over into a gold-capped cut-glass atomizer whenever it starts to run low.

As I brushed her hair, Grandma seemed to slip into a trance, her hands gently clasped on the tabletop, her eyes drifted peacefully shut. I worked quietly, studying her face. It always shocked me to see how much she'd aged, especially since Grandpa's death. It was as though her whole body, like her house and her thoughts, was turning inward. Except for the ticking of the clock, the world was perfectly silent. I laid the brush down and ran my fingers through Grandma's hair, pressing her head to my chest as my love for her swelled inside.

Over the years I've had a few boys for friends, but I've never had a boyfriend. I think about it, though. I think about what it is to be overcome with passion. And I imagine my emotions would echo what I feel when I'm alone with Grandma—brushing her hair, all my senses filled to overflowing, a perfect peace. I cleared my throat and changed position, ashamed of the tightening in my abdomen.

The shrill intrusion of the ringing telephone star-tled me, but did not cause a flicker of response on

Grandma's face. I moved swiftly across the room to silence it.

"Hello?"

"Hello, Caroline? It's Mom. Dad said I'd find you there."

"Oh. Yeah. Hi, Mom." I pulled two long, gray hairs from the front of my jeans and let them drift to the floor.

"So, listen," Mother said, "did you have a good day?"

"Um, hmm . . . it was fine. . . ."

"Good," Mom said. "How's Grandma?"

Grandma was still sitting in the same position as when I'd left her to answer the phone. "Oh, pretty good. She's been making applesauce."

"Oh, no!" Mother laughed. "Don't eat any of it. Heaven only knows what's in it."

My shoulders stiffened. "Well, what did you want?"

"I'll be finishing up here at work in about a half hour, and I was wondering if you'd like to go out and do a little shopping. You haven't bought a thing to wear to school yet this year."

The telephone cord was tangled and I gave it a little tug in a vain attempt to straighten it. "I don't really need anything."

"Well," Mom answered, "maybe you don't *need* anything, but I thought you might *want* something."

"I don't think we can really afford anything right

22

now. Besides, there's not really anything I want."

"Caroline," Mother said, her voice edged with exasperation, "this is really not a normal conversation."

"What do you mean?"

"I mean that you should *want* to buy some new clothes. Every teenage girl likes to buy new clothes. And you certainly should not be worrying about what we can and can't afford. Good grief! Why do you always have to carry the weight of the world around on your shoulders? Can't you just relax and enjoy these years a little bit?"

"I am enjoying them," I said defensively.

"Oh, Caroline," Mother said, her voice softening. "I wish you would just let your guard down. You're so protective about yourself. And about everything. You have too many rules. I just hate to see you miss out on so many things."

Grandma stirred in her chair. "Mom, can't we talk about this later?" I asked. "I was just in the middle of brushing Grandma's hair. . . ."

"Yes . . ." Mother agreed with obvious reluctance. "We can talk about this later. We can talk about this from now until doomsday, and I doubt if it would do any good. Sometimes I think you were born into the wrong century, my darling daughter."

I pressed my feet firmly against the floor and sighed more loudly than I'd meant to.

"Well, listen," Mom continued, "you don't have to go shopping if you don't want to. . . ."

"I don't."

"Okay. You don't. Well, listen. I'm going to let you go. I still have some work to do. We'll probably eat around seven, so I'll see you then."

"Okay. 'Bye."

"Good-bye. Say hello to Grandma for me."

"I will. 'Bye."

"Bye-bye."

I replaced the receiver and tiptoed back to the table. As I placed my hand on Grandma's shoulder, she awoke with a start.

"I chased them off with my broom," she said.

"Who, Grandma?" I once again ran my hands through her hair and massaged her temples.

"Those men! Those filthy men who been building houses out on the farm."

I paused and pressed the brush against my chest. "You mean they came up on your property?"

"Not exactly. They were setting on the edge, though. Under the peach trees. The whole bunch of them, setting there eating their lunch. And let me tell you, they were all making eyes at the Concord grapes that grow along the fence. So I run out and shook my broom at them and told them they'd best move along."

"I . . . I don't understand, Grandma. If they weren't actually on your property . . ."

"They weren't on my property, girl, they were in my shade!" she said angrily. "They come onto the land and chop all the trees down, but when it's their turn to rest a bit, they come up and sit in my shade." Grandma shook her head. "That don't seem right. Don't seem right at all."

I smoothed Grandma's hair and began weaving it back into a braid. "I'm sorry, Grandma."

"Well, you're not the only one. If your Grandpa knew what was happening, he'd roll right over in his grave."

The thought of Grandpa rolling over in his grave sent a shudder through me. So did the thought of Grandma chasing the workmen off with her broom. I couldn't bear to imagine anyone laughing at her.

"Ain't you done with my hair yet, girl?" Grandma snapped.

I coiled her braid and reached for her pins. "Just about. Mother said to say hello to you."

"Hello, Georgia," Grandma said, turning in her chair. She looked to the left, then to the right. "Where'd she go at, now? . . ."

"Mother's not here, Grandma." I gave her hair a little tug to make sure the pins were secure. "I was just talking to her on the phone, and she said to say hello to you."

Grandma stared at the table, puzzled. "Hello yourself, Georgia, wherever you are."

"Grandma, would you like me to warm some milk for you?"

Grandma stiffened in her chair. "What?" she shouted.

I cleared my throat. "Would you like some warm milk?"

Grandma's forehead creased deeply and she let her mouth fall slightly ajar. "You don't know what you're talking about, girl. You go on home now and let an old woman have some peace." Grandma shook her head disapprovingly.

I patted her arms and kissed the top of her head. "I'll be back tomorrow," I promised.

I rolled up the newspaper that was spread across the table. It was covered with brown, shriveled apple peels. After placing it in the trash, I rinsed Grandma's paring knife and checked the stove to make certain all the burners were off.

" 'Bye, Grandma!" I called.

She lifted her head up. "You still here?"

"I was just leaving. 'Bye . . ."

Grandma didn't answer. But Grandma has lived a long, long time and she can do whatever she wants.

3

My homeroom number is 245. It could so easily have been 246, but, no, it's 245. All wrong. And that just about sums up how I feel about school.

It would have been okay if it hadn't been for all the Magnum people. Because of the huge population growth, they had to build two new elementary schools and a new high school. The old high school then became a junior high—grades seven through nine— and the new high school was for grades ten through twelve. I don't know. It's all so confusing. Full of strangers.

I kept my head down as I made my way through the west wing to room 245. Once there, I slid into a desk at the rear of the room.

"Hey, Caroline! Is that you?"

I jerked my head up. The voice was one I knew but couldn't quite attach to a name. "Yes . . ."

"How come you're here?"

It was Darlene Zimmer, a girl I'd gone to school with since day one. Even though we'd been together all those years, I didn't know her very well. She was just always there, like the chalkboard and pencils.

"What do you mean?" I asked.

"I asked what you're doing here."

"Well," I mumbled, "this is my homeroom."

"It is? Oh, great! Have you been sick or something?"

I felt my face begin to flush. I opened my notebook and pretended to search through it. "No," I answered.

"You mean you've been here since the beginning of school? Geez! I never even noticed you until today!" she exclaimed.

Darlene was talking a whole lot louder than necessary.

"Well," I said quietly, "I was."

"Unbelievable!" Darlene laughed. "Do we have any other classes together?"

"I don't think so," I replied. Actually, we were in the same home economics class and English class, but

I wasn't about to say so. I suspected Darlene knew very well what classes we had together.

The tardy bell rang, and Darlene and a few other people raced to their seats.

"If everyone is ready," Mr. Loudon, our homeroom teacher, said, "we can get started. The homeroom period begins precisely at 8:10—that's in the morning. After today, anyone not in the room and seated at that time will be marked tardy."

Two girls in front of me giggled. Mr. Loudon gave them a stern look, took attendance, then walked over to the window and leaned against the sill. Just as he did, the shade rolled up noisily and clattered against the frame. Everyone burst out laughing, and several people applauded. Mr. Loudon stood expressionless until the room returned to relative quiet.

"Okay," he said, "now that the entertainment portion is over, there are a few things I'd like to bring to your attention. Again." Mr. Loudon paused and looked toward the doorway. "What can I do ya for?"

"Is this room 245?" the girl in the doorway asked. I'd never noticed her around school before.

"The one and only," Mr. Loudon said as he walked forward to greet her.

"I think this is where I'm supposed to be." The girl handed a slip of paper to Mr. Loudon. He glanced at it, then handed it back to her.

"That's correct. Come in and take a seat."

The new girl gave the room a once-over and slipped into a seat near the front. She had perfectly straight auburn hair and the creamiest complexion I'd ever seen. She would have no trouble fitting in at school. She was the type who would fit in anywhere.

"Class, this is Miss Madelyn Lindsay. Or should I say 'Ms.'?"

"You can just call me 'Maddy.'" A tiny vein stood out under her right eye.

"Where you from, Maddy?"

"Atlanta," she answered sweetly. "My dad was transferred."

"Ah, Atlanta!" Mr. Loudon said. "Home of the Hawks, right?"

Madelyn shrugged her shoulders. "I guess . . ."

Mr. Loudon sniffed. "Don't you know who the Hawks are?"

"A basketball team?" Madelyn's cheeks reddened.

Mr. Loudon threw his arms over his head. "Give the lady a gold star!" he shouted.

Everybody started sort of shifting around in their seats. It's okay if Mr. Loudon is a jerk in front of us, but when he acts like that to someone new it makes you want to jump up and clamp your hand over his mouth.

"Transferred from Atlanta," Mr. Loudon continued. He folded his hands together and cracked his knuckles. "And would your father work for 'The Big M'?" he asked.

"If you mean Magnum International, that's right," Madelyn said brightly.

Mr. Loudon bowed. "Welcome to our fair city."

Madelyn nodded and a smile popped out of nowhere. "Thank you."

"Now, back to business." Mr. Loudon cleared his throat and resumed his posture at the window. "For Maddy's sake, and also for those of you who haven't quite figured it out since school began two weeks ago, my name is Mr. Loudon. I am your very own personal homeroom teacher for the duration of your career at Lakeview High. You may have heard rumors that I'm not an easy man to get along with." Mr. Loudon paused to straighten his tie, obviously pleased with himself. "But," he continued, "not true. Naughta. I think you'll find I'm willing to be just as agreeable to you as you are to me."

Mr. Loudon sneezed, then blew his nose loudly. "Hay fever," he explained, stuffing the used tissue under his cuff.

Mr. Loudon closed the window so no more pollen could get in. "I have two announcements to make concerning the dance to be held after Friday night's football game. First, there will be chaperones stationed at all entries. Anyone with liquor on his or her breath or engrossed in conversation with a tie tack

31

will not be admitted. Secondly, your beloved school board, in all their wisdom, passed a motion put before them by upstanding members of the P.T.A. that prohibits anyone from leaving a school-sponsored function until it is over." Mr. Loudon gathered four or five sheets of paper from his desk top.

"I see some of you forgot to pick up your October calendars," he said. "That kind of stuff is not going to work here. Your instructions will be posted on the blackboard before the beginning of homeroom period. If you're not responsible enough to read and follow them, that's your tough luck."

I looked up at the blackboard. In big letters it said, "PLEASE PICK UP A CALENDAR AND TAKE A SEAT."

Well. At least I'd been smart enough to take a seat.

The bell signaling the end of the period rang out sharply, but nobody moved.

"Please proceed to your first-hour class with some semblance of dignity," Mr. Loudon instructed, "and, God willing, I'll see you all back here tomorrow. Class dismissed."

Madelyn Lindsay went right up to Mr. Loudon and started talking to him. I don't know how she dared. She must have needed to ask him something pretty important.

While Madelyn had his attention, I walked quickly

32

to his desk and snatched a calendar. I waited until I was outside in the hall before tucking it into my notebook.

Karl Alden and Grant Bradley were in the hall, too, surrounded by a group of kids. They were laughing at Karl as he did a pretty good imitation of Mr. Loudon.

When Madelyn stepped into the hall, Karl abruptly ended his act and took a few steps to the side to block her path. "So, you're a Magnum brat, right?"

Madelyn veered to avoid him and he touched her arm. "Did you say your name is Madelyn?" Karl asked.

"Uh-huh," she answered. "Everybody just calls me 'Maddy,' though."

I turned and hurried toward my English class.

Mr. Daverman, my English teacher, is really a special person. So soft and sure of himself. I think he's about twenty-five. He wears jeans a lot and plays classical music on the stereo during class. He said we could call him by his first name—Joel—but I don't think I will. It doesn't seem right to me.

Mr. Daverman greeted me at the door. "Good morning, Caroline."

"Hi," I said, slipping past him. I took a seat near the back of the classroom and opened my notebook to our homework assignment. I reread the poem I'd written and erased a little smudge mark on the corner of my paper. I was sitting right next to one of the stereo speakers and closed my eyes as a sweet mixture of guitar and lute swept through me.

"Can I have your attention, class?" Mr. Daverman was standing in front of his desk with Madelyn Lindsay at his side. "I'd like you all to meet Maddy Lindsay. She just moved here from Atlanta, so please do your best to make her feel welcome."

"Hi," Madelyn said softly.

A lot of the kids smiled, but nobody said anything back.

"Why don't you take a seat, Maddy, and we'll get started," Mr. Daverman said.

Madelyn walked to the back of the room and glided into the desk next to mine. "Hello," she whispered warmly.

Mr. Daverman pushed his hands deep into his pockets. "Maddy," he said, "our assignment for today was to write a free-form poem about something that is particularly meaningful to you. To who you are. It can be as short as four lines, but no longer than one page. You may have until Friday to complete the assignment."

Just then the record ended and Mr. Daverman flipped it over. "I'd like to have you take turns reading your poems aloud."

A huge groan went up, but Mr. Daverman ig-

34

nored it. "Darlene—let's start with you."

Darlene Zimmer's eyes widened as she jumped to her feet. "Now?" she asked stupidly.

Mr. Daverman nodded.

She fumbled when she first began reading it, but then became completely engrossed in her recitation. Her poem was about clothes! She read on and on and on, pausing occasionally to laugh at her own cleverness. She must have written her poem in the tiniest letters imaginable to fit it all on one page.

The next person read a really short poem about football. We continued around the room. Most of the poems were pretty short. A couple of them were funny, but a lot were about love or freedom. I could feel my hands grow clammy as my turn approached.

As soon as the boy in front of me had finished his poem and sat back down, I started to read mine.

"The moon ri—"

"Excuse me. Excuse me, Caroline," Mr. Daverman interrupted. "Would you please stand and raise your voice a bit?"

I glanced up at Mr. Daverman and managed a weak smile. It didn't seem like the room had been this quiet while the other kids were reading. Maybe it was because the music had stopped. My legs felt rubbery and I had to keep one hand on the desk for support. I cleared my throat.

"The moon rises up like a threatening fist
As the dark clouds gather to soothe him.
There was a time when the moon was a constant
    poem;
Then those men came to burn a perfect hole
And bounce, bounce, bounce across his surprised
    face.
If you remember this you should understand.
If you remember this you can understand
Why I turn low the death hum of the vacant TV
And listen with all my might
To the sound rain makes against flowers."

Just as I finished, the bell rang and everyone jumped up to leave. Mr. Daverman was staring out the window and didn't seem to notice class was over.

As I sank heavily into my seat and started gathering my things together, I became aware of a presence pressing in. It was Madelyn.

"I really liked your poem," she offered.

I ran my thumb along the seam of my notebook. "Thanks."

Madelyn looked at the class schedule in her hand. "Looks like I have biology second hour in Room 212. Is that anywhere near your next class?"

"It's a few doors down." I almost had to nudge Madelyn out of the way in order to stand up.

"Great!" she said. "Let's walk together."

I smiled and shrugged my shoulders. "Okay. . . ."

The hallway was jammed with kids, but that didn't seem to distract Madelyn. She zeroed in on me. Well, actually, she didn't ask me very many questions, but she sort of gave me a two-minute capsule of "Madelyn's Life in Review." Too much to really absorb, except that she'd lived in a lot of different places, that she'd moved here three days earlier with her parents and younger brother, and that she knew she was going to love it here.

"Have you ever seen *Ghostbusters*?" Madelyn asked when we arrived at Room 212.

"I don't know," I said. My head was still swimming with all her facts. "What are they?"

Madelyn's face looked as puzzled as I felt. "Huh?"

"I don't know what ghostbusters are," I explained.

"Oh, I see!" Madelyn laughed. "*Ghostbusters* is the name of a movie with Dan Aykroyd and Bill Murray. I take it you haven't seen it."

"Ah, no." Most people were already in their classrooms, and I was worried about being tardy. "I don't really go to movies."

Madelyn caught my eye. "How come? Don't you like them?"

"What?" I asked. "Movies?"

"Yes." Madelyn smiled. "Movies."

"I don't know. I—I guess. Well, sort of. Sometimes. I've never really gone to many." I gestured toward my classroom. "I better get going."

"Okay," Madelyn agreed. "I'm glad I got to meet you."

"Me, too," I blurted. "Well, what I mean is you. I'm glad I got to meet you. You know. Not that you got to meet me. Well"—I paused for air—"I'm glad of that, too. Actually," I added brilliantly.

Madelyn grinned and rustled the schedule she was holding. "I'll probably see you later today."

"Uh-huh."

" 'Bye!" Madelyn waved and disappeared into Room 212.

4

"Hi!" Mother glanced up at the clock. It was a little after four. "Did you stop at Grandma's on the way home?"

"Hi. No, I'm going over there in a little while." I lifted my ponytail so the air could cool and dry the back of my neck.

"How come it took you so long to get home?" Mother blew on her freshly painted nails.

"Oh, I don't know. I decided to walk home today."

"You had a telephone call!" Mother sang.

I snapped a paper towel from the holder and dabbed

at the perspiration on my forehead. "Who was it?"

Being careful not to smudge her nails, Mother straightened the slip of paper in front of her. "A girl named 'Patty Lindsay'?"

I sucked my cheek in and bit down on it. "Oh. No. Maddy Lindsay. Madelyn."

"Oh, what a darling name! Is she a friend of yours?"

"No. Not really," I answered. "She's new at school. I just met her today. She's in some of my classes. What'd she want?"

"I don't know." Mother slid the paper across the table toward me. "Here's the number. She wants you to call her back."

I picked the paper up and pressed it into my pocket. "Okay. Thanks."

"She sounded really sweet," Mother continued.

"Um, yeah. I don't really know. I just met her." I chose a brightly polished apple from a wicker basket on the kitchen counter and bit into it. "Why are you home so early?" Mother didn't usually return from work until at least five-thirty.

She tightened the cap on her bottle of fingernail polish and gave it a little shake. "I have to go back in tonight to supervise the stock boys. We're getting more and more of our Christmas merchandise in every day, and I really feel someone should be there to help them organize it all. So! I decided to take the afternoon off!"

40

The apple I was eating was quite tart. I shook some salt over the exposed flesh and sucked on it.

"Oh!" Mother beamed. "I have to tell you what happened today!"

"What?" I asked eagerly, happy the subject had turned further away from Maddy Lindsay.

"Well, I stopped in at the grocery store on my way home from work to pick up a few things, and my bill came to seven dollars and seventy-seven cents!"

"Um-hum," I coaxed.

"So the woman at the checkout counter said I should buy a 'Lucky Seven' lottery ticket."

I sat down in a chair across from Mother and brushed away some flecks of dust on the table in front of me. "So did you?"

"Yes! I'd never bought one before, but I just couldn't resist the impulse. It was such a coincidence that my total was three sevens! And they only cost a dollar. So I bought one and opened it up." Mother's hands went through the motion. "And guess what I won!"

"Seven dollars and seventy-seven cents?"

"No! I won a free lottery ticket! So I opened that one and found I'd won *another* free ticket!" Mother laughed delightedly.

"Did you open that one?"

"Um-hum. And on that one I won five dollars!"

Judging from the way she was acting, you would have thought she had won five thousand.

"By this time, though," she continued, "the carts were starting to pile up behind me—I was in the express lane—so, instead of buying five more tickets, I just took the money. Isn't that a riot?"

I smiled and agreed, but Mother was so pleased with herself I don't think she heard me.

"I quintupled my investment!" She laughed. "Quintupled. Is that right?"

Many people have told me I look like Mother, but her presence is so lively and animated, the only time I can see the resemblance is when she's reading or concentrating on something.

My earliest memories of Mother are regular. She was just constant. A warm spot. But then, when I was about eight or nine, she started to change. She cut her hair and learned to blow dry it, experimented with makeup, bought and read practically every women's magazine she could get her hands on, and she went back to school to get a degree in merchandising. Then, a few months ago, she stepped right into the job at Klugg's. I'm happy for her, but my memory of her doesn't seem to gel with the reality of her.

"Well, what do you think? Do you think I should buy five more lottery tickets the next time I'm in the store?"

I shrugged my shoulders. "I think you should keep the money."

"Oh-ho-ho," Mother said, sobering slightly. "You

are your father's daughter, aren't you. Never take a chance."

I slid my chair back. "Well, I think I'd better go to Grandma's now."

"Aren't you going to call your friend?" Mother's gaze was intent.

I patted the message in my pocket. "Oh, I'll call her later."

The phone rang, and, as Mother rose to answer it, I made my getaway. "I'll see you later tonight," I called.

Mother waved her hand in return as she picked up the receiver.

I ran out the door and jumped on my bike, pumping as hard as I could in case the caller was Madelyn. As soon as the house disappeared from view, I stopped and knelt down on the shoulder of the road. The message from Madelyn burned in my pocket. I dug a hole with a sharp stone, pulled out the message, and, without reading it, stuffed it into the hole and buried it, patting the earth down firmly. I didn't know what Madelyn Lindsay wanted from me, and I didn't care.

Madelyn Lindsay could move into my town and into my school and into my classes, but there was no way she was going to move into my life. I pressed the stone I'd used for digging into the surface of the freshly overturned earth. That was the end of that.

I brushed the dirt off my hands and knees and

pushed my bike the rest of the way to Grandma's.

Old Bill was sleeping so soundly he didn't even hear me as I wheeled my bike past him. Several flies were buzzing around his hindquarters. His tail automatically lifted and swatted them away.

The only sound to greet me inside Grandma's house was the ticking of the clock. "Grandma?" I called softly. The house seemed darker than usual. I flipped the switch of the fluorescent light above the kitchen sink, and it hummed and hesitated before springing to life. "Grandma?" I called again.

The breakfast and lunch dishes were unwashed and piled in the sink. That was not like her. A little knot of fear twisted inside. "Where are you, Grandma?" The apprehension in my own voice scared me. A scraping noise sounded from above.

I moved quickly through the house and hesitated at the foot of the stairs. "Are you up there, Grandma?"

Grandpa had been bedridden during the final months of his life, and the parlor on the main floor was converted into a bedroom so it would be easier for Grandma to care for him. The very day he died, Grandma closed off the upstairs and moved into the parlor bedroom. Several months passed before we could convince her to change the sheets on Grandpa's bed, but, even then, she still kept them unwashed and neatly folded under her pillow.

The darkness of the stairwell sent a chill through

me. After calling out a few more times, I took a deep breath and bounded up the stairs by twos. The doors leading into the three bedrooms were closed, and all but one were locked. I opened it and peered in. "Are you in here, Grandma?"

Again the scraping noise sounded from above. I glanced around the room, and, through the window, spotted a wooden extension ladder propped against the house.

I raced down the stairs and out the door. "Grandma!" I shouted. Standing at the base of the ladder, I could sense a slight movement on the roof. I climbed the ancient ladder slowly as it groaned under my weight. Once at the top, I could see Grandma standing on the roof. There was a pail beside her, and she was spreading something on the roof with a spade. She was dressed in what she considered her "good" outfit—a gray flannel suit with a yellowed white silk blouse. She had black leather pumps on her feet, and her hair was hidden under a gray felt hat with a black velvet band.

Not wanting to startle her, I hoisted myself up on the roof and called to her in a clear, low voice. "Grandma . . ."

"Who's there?" she answered pleasantly, not bothering to turn from her task.

"It's Caroline, Grandma."

"Oh." She paused. "It's you. Now's a nice time to

come. When I'm pretty near finished tarring the roof."

"Grandma, why are you doing this?" I asked, inching toward her.

" 'Cause the roof leaks, girl. Why do you think?" She plunged her spade into the bucket and quickly spread the tar she'd drawn out.

"Here," I said as I slowly stood, "let me help you with that."

"No, no," she replied. "Just one more patch and I'll be through. Been working on it since morning. Except for the few minutes I took for lunch." She spread the remaining bit of tar, then leaned heavily against her spade. "That ought to do it," she said proudly.

"Let's get down from here, Grandma," I ordered. There was hardly any tar left in the bucket, so I took it and the spade and tossed them over the edge of the roof to the ground. "Come on, Grandma. I'll go down first."

We slowly descended the ladder. I stopped and braced myself as she took each step, sure she was going to slip. The veins in her legs showed clearly through her stockings, and her whole body trembled with the strain.

When I reached the ground I put an arm out to assist her. "Grandma! Why didn't you ask someone to do that for you!"

She ignored my offer of help and turned away.

" 'Cause there ain't no life in having someone else do your living for you."

I followed her weary trek into the house. As she sank down into a chair at the kitchen table, I lit the burner under the teakettle.

"Would you like me to fix you some supper, Grandma?"

"No, no, no. A cup of tea is all I'll be needing. It don't take much food to keep an old lady going."

Knowing better than to argue with her, I silently took a cup from the cabinet and placed the day's tea bag in it. Grandma has three cups of tea a day, using the same bag for all three cups.

Grandma pulled a long pin from her hat before removing it. She placed the hat in the center of the table, then clasped her hands together and rested them in her lap.

"Grandma? Why are you dressed like that?"

She straightened the lace on her collar before answering. "In case I fell."

"What do you mean?"

"Off the roof," she answered brusquely. "I didn't want to look like a dang fool if they had to come cart me away."

The teakettle whistled rudely. I switched off the gas and poured the bubbling water over the bag in her cup.

"Be careful," I warned her. "It's hot. Are you sure

I couldn't at least fix you a piece of toast, Grandma?"

"No, sir," she continued, "nobody's going to make a fool out of me." Grandma stirred a half teaspoon of sugar into her tea. "You wouldn't let that happen, Caroline, would you?"

"No, Grandma," I promised. "Never." I kissed the top of her fragrant head.

Grandma's arms were still shaking from being tired, and tea splashed over the rim of her cup as she brought it to her lips. "I hope I die tonight," she said pleasantly.

"Grandma! Don't talk like that. You're just tired."

"No, no. It's true. I wish the same thing every night. That I'll just go to sleep and wake up in heaven."

"Grandma!" I said stiffly, giving her shoulders a shake. "Why are you talking like this?"

"Because I can still take care of myself, girl. I can still put in a day's work without nobody helping me. And that's the way I want to go out. Not ever having been a burden."

"Grandma," I whispered, "taking care of you would never be a burden."

But she was lost to me, the expression on her face a million miles away. Serene.

I didn't know where Grandma's thoughts had taken her. I only knew I wished I could go with her.

5

"Group four will be Marla Gibson, Caroline Warner, Karl Alden, Madelyn Lindsay, Mark Adler, Rita McCall, and Darlene Zimmer." Mrs. Wagner, my home economics teacher, was dividing the class into four groups. We were going to make biscuits.

My breath caught in my throat as she read the names off. So far that day I'd been able to avoid Madelyn, but it looked as though we were going to be forced together.

Darlene thrust her hand in the air and urgently

waved it. "Couldn't I be in group three instead?" she whined. "Please?"

"There will be no changing from one group to the other," Mrs. Wagner answered wearily. "If I did it for you, Darlene, I'd have to do it for everyone."

Darlene put her hand down. "Aaw . . ."

Mrs. Wagner straightened the top of her apron. I don't know how old Mrs. Wagner is. Somewhere between forty and ninety, I'd guess. She's six feet tall, skinny as a rail, and balding to the point of embarrassment. She always wears nurse's shoes, which look like they're about a size 12½ AAAAA. Her feet literally swat the floor when she walks.

Mrs. Wagner sharply clapped her bony hands. "Please, class. Take your places at the proper work station. The recipe we'll be following today is posted there, and you may assign one person to come to me for the ingredients."

There was a lot of noise as we all pushed our chairs back from the tables and assembled in the assigned work areas.

Each of the four work stations had a small stove and oven, a sink, an overhead cabinet, a lower cabinet, a drawer, and approximately three feet of counter space.

I lingered in the background as my group gathered.

"Let's move along, class," Mrs. Warner ordered.

"We only have forty minutes left, and everyone must wash his hands before we can begin."

The remaining kids hurried to their stations and lined up at the sinks. I took my place at the rear of the line behind Darlene Zimmer. Our line seemed to move more slowly than the others, and I was the only person who hadn't washed when Mrs. Wagner started rapping her desk with a wooden spoon. "Class! Class! As soon as everyone is ready, we'll begin."

I could feel her eyes and everyone else's burning into my back. I rinsed my hands and quickly dried them on a paper towel. Mrs. Wagner kept tapping her spoon the whole time.

"Now, then," Mrs. Wagner said. "I'd like one person from each group to come to me for the ingredients."

Rita snatched up the tray. "I'll do it." Nobody argued with her.

As Rita left, Madelyn moved closer to me. "Didn't your mom tell you I called?"

I stiffened. "Well, she did, but she, she wasn't sure, um, I didn't know . . ."

Madelyn smiled. "It's okay. I just wanted to ask if I could copy down the poem you wrote for English. I think about stuff like that, too, but I never seem to be able to put it in writing. At least not in so few words. Anyway, it would mean a lot to me if you'd let me copy it."

51

"Oh," I said, shifting my weight from one foot to the other.

Just then Rita returned with her tray of ingredients. Saved by the bell.

"Has everyone found the biscuit recipe?" Mrs. Wagner shouted above the din.

It would have been a real trick not to find the biscuit recipe, as it was taped to the front of the upper cabinet door in each work station. Several people mumbled that we had.

"Good," Mrs. Wagner said. "Now. I'd like every member of your group to have a hand in today's project, so decide among yourselves who will be doing what." Mrs. Wagner brushed at the front of her apron. "Quietly!" she barked.

"So," Madelyn said. "Could I?"

"Could you what?" Our first instruction was to set the oven at four hundred degrees, which I quickly did. I got a large mixing bowl from the cabinet and set it on the counter.

Madelyn poured the flour, salt, and baking powder into the bowl and began mixing them together. She raised her eyebrows at me. "Copy your poem down . . ." she repeated. "If it's too personal, that's okay. Just tell me to bug off."

"No, it's not. You can copy it. If—if you want." The next thing you know, she'll be asking for a lock of my hair, I thought.

"Move aside! Move aside, please." Karl Alden was making his grand entrance. I was glad for his intrusion.

"Oh, no," Rita said. "Now all hell is going to break loose."

Karl sniffed and thrust his chin into the air as if he'd been deeply wounded. "When my kitchen expertise knocks your socks off, Rita, I'm not going to throw that comment back in your face." Karl squinted at the instruction sheet. "What am I supposed to do?" he asked.

A couple of the kids laughed.

"You're supposed to cut the shortening into the flour mixture," Darlene instructed him.

"Your vast knowledge humbles me," Karl quipped.

Madelyn was sticking to me like glue. "When can I, then? You know. Copy the poem. Are you doing anything after school?"

"What? Today, you mean? Oh. No. I mean yes. Well, what I mean is—no I can't, because yes, I have other plans." I quickly turned my attention back to Karl.

Karl scraped shortening from the measuring cup into the bowl, took an egg whip from the drawer and proceeded to jab away at the bowl's ingredients. Flour went flying in all directions, and the shortening got all clogged up in the whip.

"This stupid thing!" Karl muttered, tapping the egg

whip on the side of the bowl. "How could anyone expect a gourmet cook such as myself to perform with these inferior tools?" When tapping the tool didn't help, he gave it a hard slam. The bowl tipped over and about half the ingredients spilled onto the counter-top. Everybody in the group laughed, and I smiled. I couldn't help it.

In a flash Karl righted the bowl, held it at counter height, and brushed the ingredients back into it with his bare hands.

"Nobody saw that, right?" He chuckled.

"I saw it," said a stern voice.

We all turned to see Mrs. Wagner standing behind us, hands on hips.

"Exactly *what* is going on here?" she asked.

"It wasn't my fault," Karl protested. "I couldn't get this stupid pastry blender to work!" He held up the egg whip, and a glob of shortening fell pathetically into the bowl.

"You couldn't get the pastry blender to work," Mrs. Wagner said, tapping her foot, "because you are not *using* a pastry blender. You are using an egg whip!"

"Oh!" Karl shrugged. "No wonder it wouldn't work."

Several people giggled, but I kept myself in the background.

"No wonder, indeed!" Mrs. Wagner said. "And none of you knew the correct tool to use?"

Nobody answered her.

"What do you think we've been studying every day for the past two weeks?"

Still no answer.

Mrs. Wagner looked straight at Madelyn.

Madelyn put her hand to her neck. "I haven't even been here that long," she offered.

"Well, come on!" Mrs. Wagner said impatiently. "Surely one of you must know. Marla?"

"We . . . we've been studying kitchen tools? And, and how's best we should use them?" Marla said.

"That's right. And could someone please identify a pastry blender? Darlene?"

Darlene opened the drawer and pulled out a pastry blender. "This?"

"Right again," Mrs. Wagner said. "Karl, please continue with the correct tool. Be sure to remove as much shortening as possible from the egg whip, or the biscuits won't turn out."

Karl began digging at the shortening with his finger. "Yes, ma'am."

"*Not* with your hands! *Never* with your hands! Use a rubber spatula!" Mrs. Wagner's mouth was drawn up tight.

Karl looked around, confused. Rita quickly handed him a spatula. "This is a spatula. . . ."

Karl grabbed it from her. "I know that's a spatula," he said indignantly.

"You may continue." Mrs. Wagner wrote something down and moved on to the next group.

I let out my breath, unaware until then that I'd been holding it. Madelyn had her back to Karl. "He's such a jerk," she whispered.

When Karl finished blending the dough, Mark added the milk and stirred it into a ball.

"I'll knead the dough," Marla said. Marla has a southern accent, and I love to hear her talk. "Y'all think I should put some more flour on the countertop before I begin?" she asked. There was still a lot of flour left over from Karl's accident.

"Put a little more down," Darlene decided.

Marla spread some flour around and took the dough from the bowl. "Don't y'all worry," she soothed. "I been making bread since I's about four years old. I love to knead the dough."

Madelyn had a look on her face like she was about to faint. She turned her head toward my ear. "Did you see her fingernails?"

I nodded. Watching Marla work was pretty sickening. Even though we'd all washed our hands, both of Marla's nails on her pinky fingers were very long and very filthy. As she pushed and pulled at the dough, little streaks of dirt appeared and were blended in. I looked at Madelyn and grimaced.

Mrs. Wagner was hanging around, so we were all silent.

It was Darlene's job to roll out the dough and cut

it into circles. She pushed at it with the rolling pin, and the dough got stuck to the underside. She scraped it off with the spatula. "I probably should have put some flour on the rolling pin. . . ."

"Brilliant deduction." Karl sneered.

Darlene shot Karl a dirty look but didn't say anything.

"He's got to be high on something." Madelyn grinned.

"His dad is a policeman," I said, "so he probably has access to all the best stuff."

Madelyn put a hand to her mouth to stifle a laugh.

Darlene had finished cutting out the biscuits and was sliding the pan into the oven. She hadn't really done a very good job rolling the dough. Some of the biscuits were thick, some thin.

Mrs. Wagner peered over my shoulder. Her breath smelled like clove. "Your biscuits are lopsided, Darlene."

"Sorry," Darlene said softly.

Mrs. Wagner turned to walk away. "They won't bake evenly," she warned.

Darlene shut the oven door with a bang. Karl was staring at her with his arms out in front as if he was measuring something.

"Mrs. Wagner's right, Darlene," he observed. "Your biscuits are lopsided."

Darlene whipped around to face him. "So are yours!" she retorted.

"Ooh, what a comeback," Karl said, clasping his heart.

The other kids laughed, but Madelyn pressed against me. "I have the feeling we're going to be the first kids in the history of the world to flunk elementary biscuit making."

I groaned and closed my eyes.

We started cleaning up while the biscuits baked. I wet a cloth while Madelyn attempted to brush the flour into a pile with her hands. I held the trash container level with the counter so she could sweep the flour into it.

Karl was jabbering away in the background. He was trying to get everybody to stare at Mrs. Wagner's feet to see what she would do. Rita, Mark, and Marla were snickering and hanging on his every word. Darlene was off to the side pouting.

Madelyn sighed. "Sometimes I feel so out of place. . . ."

I stopped wiping the countertop. "You do?" I asked. "But, but I thought you said you were going to like it here."

Madelyn slapped at the flour on the front of her jeans. "Well, I do. It's not that, really. I don't know. I guess I just feel out of place on earth sometimes."

I made wide swirls with the cloth. Madelyn touched me.

"I'm sorry. That was a dumb thing to say. Just a fleeting thought, really. Sorry."

I shrugged my shoulders, but could not help smiling. "That's okay."

Darlene was standing next to the oven with her arms folded, and, when the timer went off, she took the biscuits out and set them on the stove top. Our biscuits were the last to finish baking.

Mrs. Wagner swooped over like one of Pavlov's dogs at the sound of the bell. Some of the biscuits were burned and smelled bitter, while the thicker ones looked gooey. "I told you they wouldn't bake evenly," Mrs. Wagner reminded us. "You may each have one if you like."

Everybody took a biscuit to prove to Mrs. Wagner that they thought they were wonderful. Well, everybody except Madelyn and me. We didn't want one because of—you know—Marla's fingernails. You never knew what could be in there.

When the bell rang, we all hurried to get our books and leave. It was the last class of the day.

"See you tomorrow," Madelyn said.

I piled my books on top of my notebook, taking special care to align the edges. Something was happening to me. I could feel a little pulsing in the pit of my stomach. "Okay, Maddy." I nodded warmly. And I meant it. I honestly did.

I wrapped my arms around my books, and, with my head low, pressed them tightly to my chest. Outside the school the sky was so clear and so blue I could not bear to think of getting on the bus. I decided to walk home instead.

Although the day was sunny and bright, the air was cooler and drier than it had been. I walked briskly along and savored the moment. I felt light. In fact, I was practically home before I was even aware of myself or my surroundings. When I passed by Grandma Warner's house I detoured to the south.

There was a place I suddenly craved to be.

6

Grandpa and I had had such a special place in the orchard. I'd wanted him to be buried there.

It was a place like no other. A heaven on earth if ever there was one. On the south side of the orchard a cove had formed (or, perhaps, Grandpa had planned it that way) where the peach trees ended and the apple trees began. It was usually sunny in the cove, and a constant, gentle breeze flowed through it even on days as still as a picture. And the smell! It could not possibly have come from the earth. It was a blend of everything good and pure, and it washed over you and filled all your senses. Grandpa and I went to the cove often. We'd lean against a tree trunk, and he'd put his arm around me. Sometimes he'd braid weeds and flowers together to make jewelry for us to wear. We rarely spoke a word. We were kings of the universe.

My breathing quickened as I drew near to the spot, and when I finally arrived a thousand memories weakened my knees. I had to sit down on one of the stumps where the trees had been. The land had been cleared, but nothing had been built there yet. Beyond the cove I could see the cement slabs left from where the migrant housing had stood.

The same people came year after year to help at picking time. They were very loyal to Grandpa Warner. I especially liked one of the families. Fernando and Rosalita. They had five or six children. It always seemed like Rosalita had one baby or another strapped to her as she worked. She never minded if I hung around her. Sometimes she'd let me have dinner with them. I don't know how I knew it was okay, since neither she nor Fernando spoke any English. Rosalita and I just had an understanding between us. I loved helping her take care of the endless babies. And I loved their food. Everything spicy and cooked in oil— even the vegetables.

The cove looked so different now. I wrapped my arms around myself and tried to recall the way it had been. I also recalled how the beauty of the place had nearly been destroyed for me.

I'd been so young then—seven or eight, maybe, and had been playing in the cove all morning. I'd found some Indian arrowheads and was using them to play tic-tac-toe in the dirt. A sound startled me. It had come from the direction of the peach trees. I listened for a full thirty seconds, but, hearing nothing further, went back to my game.

After some time had passed, a strange feeling— like a tickle—started running up and down my spine and made the little hairs on the back of my neck stand on end. Someone or something was watching me. I got to my feet and glanced around.

"Frankie? Queenie?" I called anxiously.

Frankie and Queenie were Grandpa's German shepherds. They were guard dogs. I could never understand how they got to be so mean, with Grandpa loving them and all. Grandpa had trained them to respond to nearly imperceptible hand signals. They respected and obeyed only him. Anyone else they would have torn apart. When they weren't under his direct command, Grandpa kept the dogs in a steel pen with barbed wire laced along the top of the twelve-foot walls. I used to tease them once in a while, by running a stick along their pen. They'd flatten their ears and bare their teeth and growl. But no matter what I did to those dogs, they would never, ever dare hurt me. Grandpa wouldn't allow it. If Grandpa was around.

"Grandpa?" I called hopefully. No answer. I stood still, straining to hear the slightest movement. Perspiration formed along my upper lip and I licked it. "Is that you, Grandpa?"

It had to be the dogs. Maybe they'd dug a hole underneath the pen to gain their freedom. Maybe Grandpa was miles away. "Good doggies," I called in an attempt to right my wrongs. I felt movement closing in on me from behind. "You're good doggies!" I screamed.

"Señorita? It is me. Juan."

I turned toward the voice.

Juan smiled at me. "Did you think Juan was dogs of Big Boss?" he asked in halting English.

Juan was the oldest son of one of the migrant families who helped us with the harvest.

I shrugged my shoulders and bent to swoop up the arrowheads. Juan reached out and took hold of my hair. "Very pretty," he said. Any relief I'd felt over Juan appearing instead of the dogs quickly vanished when I looked at his face.

I pulled my ponytail from his grasp and tried to move away, but Juan grabbed me from behind. "Let go of me!" I shouted.

Juan's smile deepened. He had a tooth missing in front. "No, no. Juan not let you go. Juan want to play with pretty señorita. You will do what Juan says, or Juan will feed you to the dogs."

"You let go of me, or I'll tell my grandfather!" I threatened.

"No, the señorita must not tell Big Boss. If she tell Big Boss he will make Juan go away. Poor Juan. But before Juan go, he will throw pretty señorita in dog pen. Then she will not be so pretty. Poor señorita."

His arms were crushed tightly around my chest and his breath was sticky on my neck. I gathered my strength and kicked his shin with my heel. Juan dug his fingernails into my chest and popped two buttons on my shirt as I tore myself loose.

"Aha!" he laughed. "Juan like to play rough, too!"

I started to run but had only gone about twenty feet before Juan tackled me. He pressed his sweaty body over mine, pinning me to the ground. "Why don't you tell Juan how much you love him?" he said huskily.

Just then a giant shadow fell over the cove, and there stood Grandpa Warner. All one hundred feet of him. I could feel Juan's strength drain away. Then he leapt to his feet and ran.

Grandpa picked me up and held me in his arms.

"Juan said he would throw me in with the dogs if I didn't do what he said," I sobbed.

Grandpa placed his hand over my mouth. He carried me to a tree and sat down holding me tightly to him. "What is beautiful is always beautiful," he whispered. He smelled like the earth. "And what is perfect is always perfect." Grandpa raised my chin, but I kept my eyes closed. "Tell me the cove is beautiful," he instructed.

I held my breath.

"Tell me!" He squeezed my arm. Anger.

"It . . . it's beautiful." I choked.

"And tell me you are perfect."

I opened my eyes then. The sun shone from behind Grandpa's back, lighting a rainbow all around him.

"I'm perfect."

We sat by the tree in the cove until the late afternoon. We were the safest people in the world. My grandpa and I.

Sometime during that night I heard two gunshots, and in the morning Frankie and Queenie were gone. All Grandpa would say when I asked about them is that he'd gotten rid of them.

Well. Grandpa never told anyone about what had happened in the cove that day. I didn't, either. Mother'd noticed the scratches on my chest and the missing buttons. She'd asked if I'd been crawling through the raspberry patch, and I said yes.

Oh, I believed the cove was beautiful and always would be. I believed I was perfect and always would be. And I believed my grandfather was God.

Something wet and cold nudged my hand, pulling me back from my childhood.

Old Bill was sitting mournfully beside me. He'd snapped his heavy chain. He must have needed powerfully to be with me.

For just a moment I thought about wrapping what was left of his chain around his weary neck and pulling tight. For just a moment that thought seemed kind. I missed Grandpa more than I could bear.

The wind swirled in around my feet, but I could not feel it on my hands, on my chest, on my face. It spooked me a little. A lot. I jumped up from the stump and ran toward home. "Come on, Bill!" I called. "Let's go!"

Old Bill and I raced through the orchard. The oxygen went to my head and made me high. "We're perfect, Bill!" I shouted.

The clear sounds of Dad's clarinet greeted me as I pushed open the gate to our front walk. I closed the gate behind me to trap Old Bill in the yard. I patted his head. "You better stay out here, Poochie."

I hurried into the house. I wanted to tell Dad I loved him.

"Dad? Where are you? It's me. . . ."

The music stopped abruptly. He didn't even finish the measure. "Hi, Caroline," he said as he walked into the room.

Something about his appearance sobered me. "Dad? You're not sick or something, are you?"

"No." Dad's arms hung loosely at his sides. He was still clutching his clarinet. "Um. Upper management has decided to shut down our plant and switch the operation to the main plant in Mobile, Alabama." Dad paused and made a weak gesture with his hand. "So. I've lost my job."

Sometimes my father can smile just like Mona Lisa.

7

Twenty-two to the left, thirteen to the right, all the way around to the left . . . nine. Twenty-two minus thirteen is nine. A perfect combination. I gave the lock a tug and it opened.

I faced my locker and kept my shoulders hunched forward as I unsnapped the front of my gym uniform and slipped it off. I pressed the wrinkles out with my hands and hung it in my locker to dry before our next class. The gymnasium had been chilly at first, but Mrs. Albright had really given us a workout. I thought about taking a shower, but the shower room has a peculiar odor that conjures up a picture in my mind of athlete's foot fungus and other creepy things that might be living in there. I toweled off and patted baby powder across my chest and back instead.

"I can never get this thing to open!" The voice was Madelyn's. Her locker is six down from mine. "You'd think after being here a month I'd get the hang of it, but noooooo. . . ."

"Here. Let me try it. What's your combination again?" Jill Watson asked.

"Eighteen–four–twenty-six."

Jill skillfully spun the lock and snapped it open. "I don't know why you have so much trouble with this thing."

"I don't know why, either," Maddy said. "Thanks. Maybe I don't turn it far enough on the last number or something."

"I'll give you one more month to master Basic Lock Operation," Jill teased. "After that you're on your own."

Maddy pretended to bite her fingernails. "Please don't do this to me! I crumple under pressure."

Jill laughed, lit a stick of incense, and waved it around for a few seconds before snuffing it out. "It sure smells gross in here."

Madelyn pulled her shoes off without untying them. "You can take it, Jill."

Madelyn is friendly to everybody on the face of the earth! I'm not really jealous or anything like that. Actually, it sort of annoys me. I don't know why. I guess the fact that she's not very choosy makes me feel unspecial. Like one of many. Like I'd better be very careful about what I say around her. She's asked me to have lunch with her and her friends a bunch of times, but they always buy their lunches in the cafeteria, and I carry a lunch from home.

The cafeteria serves food I can't really recognize. It usually has either red or yellow sauce poured over the top. I always need to know what I'm eating. Also, the cafeteria is so crowded and noisy at noon, I can't make myself go in there. Indigestion City.

I dressed and started out of the locker room, doing my best to avoid Madelyn and her group. Just as I was nearing the door, the girl in front of me slipped on her way back from the shower, her backside slapping loudly against the tile floor. After a shocked moment, she burst into a gale of laughter, and several people rushed over to see what had happened.

"You okay, Megan?" Mrs. Albright asked.

Megan, still laughing, nodded her head. Since I was the closest one to her, I offered a hand to help her up.

"Thanks," she said, taking it and rising to her feet.

"I can't believe I did that. What an airhead."

"You sure you're okay, Meg?" Mrs. Albright gets pretty hyper about accidents in her class and had come closer for a better look.

"Yes. Just a little embarrassed," Megan assured her.

Mrs. Albright lifted her nose in the air and put her hands on her hips. "Is that marijuana I smell?"

You could have heard a pin drop.

Without even looking up, I knew exactly what was going to happen next.

"Caroline," Mrs. Albright demanded, "would you please tell me who's been smoking marijuana in here?"

I slouched inward and groaned. That's the thing. When you get pegged as someone who tells the truth, people are always trying to get you to tell it.

I shrugged my shoulders.

"We were just burning some incense, Mrs. Albright," Maddy said. "Sorry."

"And who is 'we,' may I ask?"

Maddy looked around. "We is . . . is me!" She giggled.

Mrs. Albright stretched out her hand. "I'll take it."

Maddy reached into Jill's locker and got the incense and a book of matches.

"I'm going to let this incident go, Maddy," Mrs. Albright decided. "But I don't ever want this stunt repeated."

"Thank you, Mrs. Albright," Maddy said. "It won't happen again."

People like Madelyn Lindsay are so charming they know in their bones they can get away with things that would probably put anyone else in prison.

Mrs. Albright's mistrust disappeared. She reached out and pinched Madelyn's cheek. "I don't know about you," she said affectionately.

Madelyn smiled her perfect smile and shrugged her shoulders.

As soon as the excitement had ended, I pushed the locker-room door open and tried to sneak out. A hand touched my shoulder and I stiffened.

"Look what I have!" Maddy sang out, swinging a small, brown paper bag. "I brought a lunch from home today so you wouldn't have an excuse not to eat with me." She smiled and patted the bag. "Okay?"

I held the door open for her. She'd trapped me. "Okay."

We didn't talk much as we moved across campus. Maddy was too busy saying hello to everyone. In just a few weeks, she had managed to know more people by name than I had in years.

When we reached the sidewalk, Maddy turned to me. "Where are we going, anyway?"

I readjusted the weight of my notebook. "Oh, there's a little park not too far from here. Just a few blocks.

Right outside the business district. There's not much to it, really, just a few benches and a goldfish pond. Only there aren't any goldfish in it. Be—because it's getting to be too cold outside for them."

"Sounds great to me!" Maddy replied. Our silence continued for a while as we walked. "So," Maddy said at last, "does your mom or dad work for Magnum, or what?"

"Um, no," I answered hastily. "They don't."

A strand of auburn hair was plastered across Maddy's lower lip. She brushed it out of the way. "Have you lived here long?"

"Um-hum. I've always lived here."

"Boy! You are a rarity!" Maddy gasped. "Where do you live?"

"Out near Whitneyville Road and Rural Route One."

"Let's see. Whitneyville and Route One . . ." Maddy closed her eyes. "Oh! I know where that is! That's right near Old Orchard Estates. I have a few friends who live there."

Near Old Orchard Estates! If she only knew! I bit the inside of my cheek and nodded.

"I've ridden home on the bus a few times with girls who live out there. How come I've never seen you?"

The day was overcast and the wind came in chilly gusts that went right through me. I pulled my notebook close. "Well, when the weather's nice like it has

74

been, I'd rather walk. It's not that far, really. Just a couple of miles."

"Oh! Do you live in that old brick house that's all covered with vines?"

"No, not really. But I spend a lot of time there. That's my grandparents' house. Well, Grandpa died a couple years ago, so just my grandma lives there now. My house is across the street and around the corner from Grandma's."

When Maddy talks to you, she stands a little closer than most people. I leaned slightly to the left.

"Hmm," Maddy said, trying to get a mental picture, "I can't place your house. Anyway, I love your Grandma's house. It has so much character! Don't tell anyone I said this, but that's one thing that sure is missing in the subdivision."

I just looked at her and smiled.

"From what I hear, this town has really undergone a change in the past five years. What was it like before?"

"It was smaller," I said. "Well, not really smaller. Just a lot fewer people more spread out. And it was quaint. There wasn't much industry or many businesses. It really wasn't much more than a farming community."

"Did you grow up on a farm?"

I hesitated. A farm girl. If I admitted it, Maddy

would probably imagine me with grimy bare feet, ripped coveralls four inches too short, a straw hat and a weed stuck between the gap in my front teeth. "Not . . . not really," I answered, "but my grandparents had a huge orchard, and I spent a lot of time there."

A few drops of rain hurled against us in the wind. Maddy tightened her sweater around her neck. "Oh, neat! Where was it?"

"Where was what?" The rain was now coming down in earnest. This was not working out.

"The orchard! Your grandparents' orchard?"

It took a moment for her question to sink in. "Right around where my grandma lives now! Right where Old Orchard Estates was built."

We'd been walking at quite a brisk pace and were almost to the park. Maddy slowed slightly. "You mean there used to be an orchard where all those houses are now?" I nodded. "Neat!" she said.

We stopped on the sidewalk when we reached the park.

"We're going to get soaked." Maddy hugged her sweater close. "And I'm absolutely freezing!"

"Me, too."

"What's that building over there?"

"That?" I asked, pointing to a large, brick structure across the street. "That's city hall."

"Let's eat in there," Maddy decided, walking toward the curb.

76

"I . . . I don't think we're allowed."

"Of *course* we are!" Maddy replied. "It's a public building, so the public is allowed to be in it. And that means us!"

Before I could object again, Maddy had me by the arm and halfway across the street.

The lobby smelled of stale air and cigarette smoke. Just to the left was a huge stairway. A sign next to it read, "MAYOR'S OFFICE—SECOND LEVEL."

"Should we sit here in the lobby?" Maddy asked.

"No—let's just go. We can sit under a tree in the park. It's not raining that hard." I could just see the mayor coming down and having us arrested for loitering.

A woman suddenly appeared from one of the offices adjacent to the lobby.

"May I help you, girls?" she asked suspiciously.

"No. We're fine," Maddy said, pulling me toward a door marked "Women."

As we entered the bathroom, the strong smell of disinfectant filled my lungs.

Maddy looked around the room. "How about in here?"

"You mean eat?" The thought of it made my stomach turn, but it was certainly better than eating in the lobby. "Well, okay. I guess so."

There was no one else in the bathroom. It must not have been a very popular lunch spot. Maddy and I settled ourselves on the floor underneath the electric hand-drying machines.

Maddy unwrapped what looked like a chicken salad sandwich on a Kaiser roll. She nibbled at a corner of it, and several poppy seeds tumbled off and clung to her sweater.

My peanut butter and jelly sandwich had somehow gotten squashed. It was pretty pathetic compared to Maddy's fancy sandwich. I cupped it in my hands as we ate.

"Do you like to read?" Maddy plucked the poppy seeds from the front of her sweater.

"Um-hum," I answered.

I love to read, but the thing is, I hadn't read a very big variety of books. The library at my elementary school was tiny. Not much bigger than a closet. For some reason, I had thought it contained a copy of every book that had ever been written, so I read the same books over and over for fear I would run out of new books to read. Even though I now know it isn't true, the pattern was set. I couldn't shake the habit of savoring and rereading and practically memorizing every book I laid my hands on.

"Yes," I said again. "I read a lot."

Maddy bit into a pear and dabbed at the juice on her chin with a napkin. "I thought so. Have you read anything by Pablo Neruda?"

I'd never heard of him, but I didn't want to admit it. "I'm not sure. The name sounds familiar. What'd he write?"

"Poetry. Really romantic poetry. I have a couple of his books you can borrow if you want." Maddy took a celery stick from a small plastic bag and crunched into it. "My sister and I used to read them together."

"You have a sister!"

Maddy stopped chewing and grinned. "Well, you don't have to act so horrified."

"Well, I mean, I guess I just never saw you with anyone. With anyone like a sister, I mean."

Maddy laughed. "Laura doesn't live here."

"You mean she still lives in Atlanta?"

"Huh-uh." Maddy crumpled her napkin. "Dallas. We only lived in Atlanta for a year. We lived in Dallas before that."

"Wow!" I said. "You sure have been around!"

Maddy knelt and brushed crumbs from her lap. "I sure have."

"So how come Laura is still in Dallas?"

Maddy was searching through her purse. "She's a senior this year. And, and when we moved to Atlanta and then here, Laura decided to stay in Dallas. 'Cause, see, she liked the school she was in. And she was really involved there. And stuff." Maddy snapped her purse shut, never having found whatever it was she'd been looking for. She ran a thumbnail over her cuticles.

"Well, do you have relatives in Dallas?"

Maddy glanced toward the door and hesitated before speaking. "No. . . . Why, uh, why do you ask?"

"Well, I, I was just wondering who she lives with," I mumbled apologetically. I don't know why I felt apologetic.

"Oh." Maddy picked a piece of lint from the front of her sweater. "She's staying with—with— Well, she just had to stay there. She's in a school. A special school. She's not really well. Laura has had a hard time." Tears glistened in Maddy's eyes. She took a deep breath and the tears vanished. It seemed like she'd had a lot of practice. "You remind me so much of Laura," Maddy said cheerily. "Laura writes poetry, too. I'll show you some of it sometime."

"I'd like that." I looked down at my arms and noticed the hair on them had somehow gotten longer and darker. I held them close to my sides. "You think we ought to be heading back?"

Maddy pulled an oversized yellow comb from her purse and ran it through her hair. "What's the rush? We have some time yet." She put the comb back and drew out a tube of pale, glossy lipstick. She ran it across her lower lip, then pressed her lips together. "Want to use it?" she offered.

I ran my teeth over my lips. They were sort of

chapped. "No, ah, no thanks. I—I don't really wear any makeup. Just sometimes I put Vaseline on my lips. Not—not very often, though." I drew my mouth up tight. This silver tongue of mine never quits.

"Aha, a natural beauty!" Maddy said. "Lucky girl."

"I guess you might call me farm-fresh." I blushed.

Maddy laughed. "Can I see that poem you wrote for English?"

"Which one? The one about the moon?"

"No, the one we had to write describing ourselves. The one you read yesterday."

I opened my notebook and flipped through it. "Okay."

Maddy moved in close as I snapped open the rings and gently lifted the poem out. I backed away slightly as I handed it to her.

She cleared her throat and rapidly read aloud:

"I'm a jolt It's a game I'm a cog in the wheel
It's a joke I'm a creak It's the things that you feel
I'm a clown It's a place I'm a knot in the rope
It's a time I'm a tear It's the things that you hope
I'm a star It's a sham I'm the snow at the pole
It's a dirge I'm a cloud It's the dark in the hole
I'm a bone It's the white I'm the hand on the
  wheel
It's the black I'm a cell It's the sum of what's real

I'm a mom It's a lie I'm a bump in the road
It's a truth I'm a child It's an awesome load
I'm a frown It's a shame I'm a cry in the night
Who's to blame I'm a smile It's a soul in flight."

Maddy let her tongue hang out and pretended she
was panting. "Wow! You're a real psycho!" She winked
and patted the top of my head.

My face reddened. "Well, I . . . I don't really think
all that stuff. I was just trying to get it all to rhyme."

Maddy squealed and hugged the poem to her chest.
"You are priceless!" She sobered a bit then. "You're
not on anything, are you?" she asked cautiously.

"On anything?"

"Yeah. You know. Uppers and downers. Pot. Al-
cohol."

"You mean drugs? No! I don't even take aspirin
for a headache! I don't even take vitamins! Why, ah,
why did you ask me that? Do—do you—you don't
take drugs, do you?"

"I've tried a few things," Maddy admitted. "It's hard
not to. It seems like practically everybody I know is
on something."

I almost said, "It does?" but stopped myself. Maddy
was probably already thinking I was naive and backward and an all-around loser. "Yeah, I know," I said.

"Why do you think they do it?" Maddy smiled.

"Ah, I don't really know. . . ." I wasn't at all prepared for Maddy's pop quiz. "Why do you?"

"There's probably a lot of reasons." Maddy shrugged. "I don't know. Well, I guess I know some things. I suspect I know about as much as you."

"I don't know anything." There was hardly any air in the bathroom. I was beginning to feel lightheaded.

Maddy blinked. "Okay . . ." Her face was pretty flushed, and she looked—I don't know—desperate or something. "It just doesn't seem like everything should be so damned hard! It seems like if there ever was such a thing as a lost generation, it has to be ours. Don't you think?"

"Ours?" I blurted. "I—I don't know. I'm not really a part of it."

"See what I mean?" Maddy laughed. "Our generation is so lost even some of the people who are in it can't find it!"

I stared at her blankly, trying to soak her in.

Maddy self-consciously put a hand to her mouth. "What's the matter? Do I have a poppy seed stuck between my teeth or something?"

I turned my full attention to her teeth and studied them. "No. I don't see any."

Maddy stood and looked in the mirror. I stood, too.

"Well," Maddy asked my reflection, "what, then?"

"No. Nothing. Nothing, really. I just couldn't get you into focus for a minute there. It—it was like you were in all different pieces," I numbly explained.

Maddy turned her eyes upward and puffed out her cheeks. She waved my poem at me. "You write a poem like this and then tell me *I'm* in different pieces?" She laughed.

Little beads of perspiration sprang up along my upper lip. I wiped them away. "No. I just . . . oh, I don't know. I'm sorry."

"Well, don't be." Maddy's smile had vanished.

"Well, I . . . I . . ." I mumbled.

"I think you and I are pretty typical, though. Don't you? Feeling like we're made up of a whole lot of different things?"

She and I? How could she possibly see us as a matched set? "I—I don't know. I guess so." The mirror reflected my serious image, and I made a conscious effort to uncrease my brow. "Yeah. I guess we are." We?

"Oh! I'm so mad at myself!" Maddy suddenly said. "You must feel like you've been hit by a tornado. I was trying not to do that."

I managed a weak smile. "Not really. . . ."

Maddy ran her fingers through her hair. "You probably think I'm a real jerk."

Maddy's remark made me smile. "Actually," I confessed, "I was thinking just the opposite."

"Really?" Maddy looked so keenly vulnerable I almost hugged her. " 'Cause I—I—well—you're just so

84

quiet and gentle and sweet, and I know I come on like a whirlwind sometimes. Well, most times." She grinned.

"I think that's neat," I quickly said.

"And I think you're neat."

The temperature in the bathroom must have been around a hundred and twenty degrees. I took a step back from Maddy.

Maddy's grin widened. "Adolescence is the pits. No doubt about it." There was a small window in the bathroom, and a sudden glint of sunlight made her lips gleam. "Oh, great! It must have stopped raining!"

"Um-hum." I nodded stupidly, staring at the ray of sun like I'd never seen one before.

Maddy scooped up the remainders of our lunch and pushed them into the trash container. "We better be getting back."

I folded my poem in half and randomly tucked it between two pages in my notebook. "We probably should," I agreed. "It must be getting pretty late."

Maddy pushed the bathroom door open and held it for me. "I like you a lot, Caroline," she said warmly. "Will you come over to my house sometime? Soon?"

"Sure," I answered. I felt alive! I could hardly believe it.

Maddy and I hardly made a sound as we crossed the vacant lobby.

8

My mother rises to occasions, and this one was no exception.

In fact, the news about Dad losing his job seemed to excite her. She was unfaltering in her belief that we'd all be fine; that she could support the family if we all did a little belt-tightening; that Dad, with his work experience, would step right into another job; that when life deals you a blow, you pick yourself up and deal it back.

Her enthusiastic optimism buoyed us up for the first few weeks. Life went on in a fairly normal fashion, except that Dad filled his days with things other than his job.

He stripped and rewaxed the kitchen floor, painted the insides of the cabinets, repaired the storm windows, scrubbed the grout between the bathroom tiles with bleach and a toothbrush, made batches of soup and bread, and washed down the floor of the garage. His pattern was to spend mornings job hunting, but, so far, he hadn't had much luck. He had had only one offer—to train as manager of a fast-food restaurant that was about to open. But Mother talked him out of it. She was positive something terrific was going to come along any minute.

In any case, although things appeared to be all right, the fact that things weren't all that rosy as far as Dad was concerned was starting to sink in.

When I was a really little girl, Dad would let me sit on his lap on hot Sunday afternoons and pull the "dead" white hairs from his bare chest. If I accidentally pulled a "live" black one, he'd howl and carry on till tears ran down my laughing face. I must have been about twelve years old before it dawned on me that hair was hair, and plucking the "dead" white ones hurt just as much as plucking the "live" black ones. You practically have to hit me over the head with the evidence before I recognize discrepancies between what I think is true and what the truth really is.

Now the truth about Dad hit me like a ton of bricks.

87

His music had stopped. Abruptly. The clarinet that had sweetened all my days had been put away.

I tried to be cheerful around Dad, and Mother did, too. But when it comes right down to it, what can you say to a person whose music has stopped?

"Throw me that hammer, will you, Caroline?"

Dad and I were spending Saturday afternoon at Grandma's house, cleaning up and getting things ready for winter.

I handed the hammer to Dad and sat down on the rickety steps of the front porch. The rotted boards were warm and pungent from the late afternoon sun. I could have stayed there for ten years. I'd let Old Bill off his chain while we worked, and he was busy sniffing and digging at a pile of scrap lumber along the side of the house.

"What you looking for, Bill?" I walked over to him and tugged the tip of his tail.

He was so engrossed in his search that he ignored me.

"What's under there, fella?"

I kicked a board over, and a weathered soup bone was revealed. Old Bill snatched it greedily and ran under some bushes in front of the house. I looked down at the board I'd overturned. In a childish scrawl it read, "Tomatoes, Apples, Peaches, Q-cumbers, Etc." A thousand memories flooded over me and I sank to my knees.

This was my sign! My breathing became ragged as I remembered how proud I had been to know how to use "Etc."

Every summer Grandpa would let me sell as much produce as I could pick. I'd get out of bed at five-thirty in the morning, pick fruits and vegetables until nine, then set myself up in front of Grandpa's house.

I would carefully display my day's "catch" on a long board supported by apple crates at each end. I did quite a business, too! Not exactly what you'd call brisk, but, still, the existence of my cut-rate produce stand was well known in town. I had many regular customers and made more than a little money.

Each week I'd buy twenty-five cents worth of candy and a "Rainbow" tablet. It was a small pad with four different colored pages. It was one-fourth blue, one-fourth pink, one-fourth yellow, and one-fourth green. In it, I wrote four short stories, each one lasting as long as the color held out. Sometimes the endings droned on and on and on; other times the stories came to an abrupt halt.

I kept the rest of the money I made in a cigar box right up on the makeshift counter and never worried about anyone taking it. When lunchtime or break time or some other distraction came along, I'd just put a cardboard sign next to the cashbox instructing my customers to "Please Pay Here." And they always did.

An untended cashbox on a board next to the road

wouldn't last more than thirty seconds now. I wrapped my arms around my legs and pressed my head against my knees.

"Caroline!" Dad's voice sounded alarmed. "Are you okay?"

"Yes," I answered without looking up. "I'm fine."

Dad hurried over to me. "What's wrong? Are you sick?"

It was no use. I couldn't stop the tears. "No, I was just thinking."

Dad put his hand on my shoulder. "About what?"

I inhaled unevenly and gestured toward the sign. "About this . . ."

"Oh, my gosh," Dad said. "That sign just about sums up your entire childhood, doesn't it?

I nodded and pressed my fingers to my temples.

"I was so proud of you." Dad eased himself down next to me. "Every morning when I drove to work, there you'd be. And every afternoon when I drove home, you'd still be there. Rain or shine, in sickness and in health. No matter what. Remember how I used to honk and wave?"

"Um-hum," I said, a huge tear spilling out and making a dime-sized wet spot on my dusty jeans. "And sometimes you'd stop and buy a piece of fruit. For a quarter! I can't believe I charged my own dad a quarter for something I got free! What a rip-off!" I said, my sobs turning to sudden, jerky laughter.

Dad patted my knee. "You drove a hard bargain, all right."

"What a nerd."

"No, no, no," Dad assured me. "Not a nerd. Just a little too much on the serious side. I used to worry about that sometimes. I still do."

I rested my head on my knees.

"What's making you sad, Caroline? Is it just the nostalgia?"

"I don't know." My voice was soft and flat. "Things have changed so much. Sometimes I wish I could go back to my childhood and live there forever."

"I know the feeling." Dad drew a wadded tissue from his pocket and dabbed at my face. "It's clean," he promised. "But you have to remember that change isn't necessarily bad. Change is just . . . change." He was quiet for a moment. "And I guess you should be thankful that you had a childhood so lovely you'd want to go back to it."

"But it all just seems so hard! And sometimes like it's not even worth it." A small stone was wedged into the sole of my shoe. I poked at it.

"What seems hard and worthless?" There was more than a little concern in Dad's voice.

"I don't know. Growing up." The pebble in my shoe worked loose. I squeezed it between my thumb and forefinger. "I guess I always thought becoming an adult would be automatic. That you just looked in the mirror one day and said, 'Hey! I have arrived!' and everything inside you would magically be settled and sure."

Dad smiled. "Well, you certainly couldn't have thought that by the example your parents have set! Look at all the changes your mother and I have gone through. When you think about becoming an adult, the key word is 'becoming.' You never really—"

"Grandpa was an adult," I cut in.

My accusatory tone caused a little dimple to appear along Dad's jaw. He smacked his lips. "I'm sure your grandpa was the best person he was capable of being."

We sat together for a while beside the pile of old lumber, the only sound coming from Old Bill gnawing on his soup bone. Finally, Dad rose to his feet and brushed off the back of his pants.

"We've got a lot of work to do, Toots." He extended a hand to pull me up. "How about hosing off the shutter leaning up against the house over there. If it's in good enough shape, I'm going to put it back up."

I hosed off the shutter and raked the debris that had collected around the house since spring clean-up. Then I swept the front porch, steps, and sidewalk. When I peeked into the house, Grandma was sound asleep, a half-completed afghan spread across her lap, crochet hook in hand. Dad and I were surprised she'd allowed us to help in the yard. When you offer to help her clean the house, she gets really offended.

"I'm afraid this shutter is a goner," Dad judged. He flaked off a few bubbled strips of paint with his thumbnail.

Dad lifted the heavy shutter and carried it to the side of the house. He leaned it against the pile of scrap lumber, then stepped back to survey the exterior of the house.

"This trim is going to need another coat of paint next spring."

"Um-hmm. I'll help you if you want," I offered. .

"Help me! And here I thought for sure you'd volunteer to do it all for your poor, old dad."

It was beginning to get dark, and Dad gathered his tools. "We'd better go home and get cleaned up. Mom's taking us out for dinner tonight."

I almost started to ask if we could afford to go out for dinner, but stopped myself in time. What a slap in the face. "Just a minute, Dad. I have to put Old Bill back on his chain."

"Come on, old boy," I said, parting the overgrowth in front of the house. All that remained of Old Bill was the indentation where he'd been.

I stiffened and looked around. "Bill? Bill? Come here, boy."

"What's the matter?" Dad asked. "Isn't he there?"

I looked once more to make sure I hadn't somehow

missed him the first time. "No! Not even his bone!"

Dad cupped his hand to his mouth. "Bill! Come on, Poochie! Come, Bill!" he ordered.

As I moved closer to where Dad was standing, Bill's destination struck us both at the same time.

"Let's go home and get the car," Dad said. "If you want, I'll go over there myself."

"No. I'll get him. I'll walk. It's not that far."

"Are you sure?" Dad's forehead creased into a dozen folds. "Because I really don't mind."

"I don't mind, either, Dad," I called over my shoulder. "I want to do it. Bill's a lot closer to me."

Dad knew not to argue. "See you back at the house!"

It was only a half mile away. I jogged the whole distance and was there within minutes. Grandpa's grave was just off the main road that ran through the cemetery, and I could see Old Bill as I rounded the corner. He looked younger. And he wagged his tail happily as I sat beside him, leaning my back against the small stone marker that read: "John August Warner, 1901–1982, To The Earth Returned."

I placed my hand on Old Bill's head. "I thought I'd find you here." A little patch of earth showed signs of having been recently overturned, and the edge of Old Bill's soup bone stuck out of it.

"You're okay, Bill," I soothed him.

John August Warner.

John August Warner colored so many of my days

the world has gone dim without him. At least half my life was spent entirely with him. Sometimes he'd let me swing on his arm as we watched over the orchard, but, usually, I was a step or two behind. And, although I was the flesh of his flesh, he made me feel I'd been somehow chosen. He rarely talked to me, nor I to him. We had entire conversations without speaking a word.

Grandpa Warner got up at the same time every day and went to bed at the same time every night. He had a small black-and-white portable TV, but the only thing he ever used it for was to watch the six o'clock weather report. On Sundays he bought *The New York Times* and read it from front to back. I guess that was all he needed to know about the world. Grandpa always drank his coffee from a yellowed porcelain cup with the stirring spoon still in it. And, because dessert was his favorite part of the meal, he always ate it before his dinner. Also, he kept a bottle of whiskey in the apple shed and took a shot in his coffee before he started his chores each day. Sometimes he'd let me have a sip. It tasted pretty rank, but I drank it anyway.

Grandpa Warner died in April of 1982 after having been sick all winter. It had been a particularly cold spring. We'd even had a blizzard on April Fool's Day! The day of Grandpa's funeral, though, was sunny and windy with temperatures in the sixties. He would have liked that. I remember thinking at the time that if

Grandpa could only have hung on until that day, he would have made it a while longer. Until the next winter. On the other hand, all the newness and promise of spring may have saddened him. He was so sick and old. Ready for harvest.

I dream of him still. I dream that I wake to find him sitting on my bed. He never speaks. He just looks at me and smiles. Sometimes I'm aware that it's a dream and try to wrench awake. He disappears. Wherever he is is far.

Old Bill groaned contentedly and rolled onto his back in an invitation to rub his chest. I ran my fingers over the sparse hair of his yellowed pink belly.

During the long, cold months of his illness, I used to sit beside Grandpa's bed in the evening while I did homework or read. One night he'd stirred and reached for me.

"Caroline . . ."

I'd stroked his arm, amazed at how thin and white it had become. My favorite old swing. "Yes, Grandpa?"

He'd closed his eyes then and drawn a shallow, ragged breath. "Have I ever told you I love you?"

"No, Grandpa. You never have."

Unmistakable sorrow had creased his face as he acknowledged his painful omission. "I'm sorry."

He'd been so still after that, I had assumed he'd fallen back into his drugged sleep. I'd just gone back to my studies when he'd turned his head toward me. "Caroline," he'd whispered.

"Yes, Grandpa. I'm here."

"You will always share my deepest thoughts."

Grandpa had insisted on wearing his wire-rimmed glasses during the day, even though toward the end he constantly drifted in and out of sleep. I'd stared down at the girl reflected in them, transfixed and deep in thought. He had said, "You will always," not "You have always . . ." Why?

"Caroline?" he'd called out again.

"Yes, Grandpa?"

"Don't follow me no more."

Old Bill nudged my leg with his nose. The wind picked up as darkness crept over the cemetery, and I hugged Old Bill close. I laid my head on his chest and listened to his heart thump-thumping away.

Part of me had died with Grandpa Warner. But, if there truly is life after death, did it follow that part of me was alive and well and living with him?

I closed my eyes. The earth was so silent I could hear it spin on its axis.

9

Seventh hour had been over for at least ten minutes, and still no sign of Maddy. The school building had emptied fast, and there were just a few stragglers passing by. It takes Maddy at least three times as long as me to do something, because she has so many distractions. I leaned against the cool brick wall of the east wing to wait.

The school was absolutely silent. What if Maddy had forgotten she invited me to her house? It'd be pretty embarrassing to admit it to Mom and Dad.

They'd been so excited about my going home with her.

Well. A few more minutes of waiting wouldn't hurt.

I hadn't realized I'd been standing beside the teachers' lounge until the door opened and a man came out. It was Mr. Loudon, my homeroom teacher. I must have jumped ten feet off the ground.

"Waiting for someone?" he asked.

"Oh, n-no . . . I . . . I was just standing here," I stupidly explained.

"Oh, I see," he said, smiling. "And is there something in particular you like about that spot?"

"Well, ah, no. I was just standing here because this is where I happened to be when I stopped," I babbled. "I, uh, and I stopped so I could start thinking about how I probably forgot something. Or something," I added wittily. My face burned.

"Oh!" Mr. Loudon exclaimed, throwing his hands up in the air. "Now I get it! Why didn't you say so in the first place?" He chuckled heartily.

I just stood there like a giant dork, staring at the ground, wishing one of us would disappear. Particularly me.

Mr. Loudon curled the end of his necktie around his finger. "Say. I've been meaning to ask you. Are you Richard Warner's daughter?"

I shook my head yes.

Mr. Loudon had rolled his tie all the way up to his collar. He let it fall back into place. "I thought I could see a family resemblance. I went to school with your Dad. He was in the class ahead of me, and I always admired him. Real fine man."

"Yes, I . . . I like him, too," I said.

Mr. Loudon grinned. "Well, that works out real well, then, considering you're in the same family and all."

I still hadn't looked at him.

We both turned our attention to rapid footsteps echoing down the corridor. It was Maddy. At last.

"Hi, Caroline!" she called as she approached. "Hi, Mr. Loudon."

"Hi, Maddy!" Mr. Loudon and I chorused.

"Sorry I'm late." Maddy smoothed back her hair. "I had to talk to Mr. Daverman about something."

"Aha! Mr. Daverman!" Mr. Loudon said. "What a perfectly lovely way to end the day."

Maddy's lips pressed together. "I like Mr. Daverman."

Mr. Loudon shifted position. "I do, too," he said in his most nasal tone. "He's a real peach. Well, I'm on my way. Tell your father hello for me." He winked.

"I will. 'Bye . . ."

"Bye-bye."

When he'd left the building, Maddy nudged me. "Let's go!"

100

The cool air took our breath away. " 'The frost is on the punkin,' " I wisely observed.

"Huh?" Maddy zipped her jacket and turned the collar up.

" 'The frost is on the punkin.' You know. The poem? By James Whitcomb Riley."

"Oh, yeah! I haven't heard that one in years! How'd you ever remember it?"

"Just lucky, I guess."

Maddy laughed. "I can't wait to tell you. I went in to talk to Mr. Daverman. Isn't he a gorgeous hunk? I go wild every time I see him!"

I nodded my agreement, although I'd never thought about a teacher in that way before.

"Anyway. I asked him if I could be on the school paper—he's faculty advisor—and he not only said yes, he gave me an assignment!"

I leaned over to look at the sheet of paper on top of her notebook, but we were walking so briskly, I couldn't get the words in focus. "What is it?"

"It's a survey, and I want you to be in it. I have to ask people what their favorite TV program is!" She laughed. "I saw Karl Alden just after I left Mr. Daverman's room, so I asked him. And you know what he said?"

"What?"

Maddy slowed her pace so she could read his exact words. "He goes, 'Selecting a favorite TV show is no

101

easy task. There are so many fine offerings to choose from, it's really difficult to narrow it down to just one. But the thing that really makes a Saturday evening at home worthwhile is when they have a special six-hour *Love Boat*.' Isn't that a scream?"

"Uh-huh."

Maddy affectionately passed her fingers over the words she'd recorded. "So what's yours?"

"What's my what?" Raindrops heavy with the promise of snow pelted down.

"Your favorite TV show!"

"Oh. No. I don't want to be in it."

"Why not?" Maddy scolded. "It's just for fun."

"I don't really have a favorite. And I can't think up anything funny."

Maddy put her pen away. "Okay. But just remember I gave you the chance to star in the school paper."

I grimaced. "Oh, no," I moaned. "And that was my biggest aspiration in life."

"I hope not," Maddy said. "Really. What *do* you want to study in college? Oh! My feet are freezing!"

I glanced down at Maddy's feet. She was wearing Docksiders with no socks. "Agriculture," I mumbled.

"Huh?"

"Agriculture!" I shouted.

"Agriculture," Maddy repeated, curling her lip. "Agriculture? You mean like chickens and cows and stuff? Why would anyone want to study that?"

102

"It doesn't only mean animals," I answered huffily. Maddy was acting like I'd just said I hoped to become a mass murderer or something. "I've been sort of thinking about having my own orchard someday."

Maddy began searching through her purse, and pulled out her pen. "How about if I say your favorite TV show is *Hee-Haw*?"

"What?" A heavy snowflake landed on my lip and I licked it off.

"Just kidding!" Maddy bubbled. "Hey! Look! It's snowing!" The temperature had dropped enough to freeze up the rain.

"Look how dark the sky is," I said.

"Oh! I hope we get a blizzard!" Maddy exclaimed. "I just adore winter! We lived in New England for a while when I was younger, and winter was always one of my favorite seasons."

"Mine, too," I said.

"Do you ski?" Maddy asked.

"No."

"Ice skate?"

"Not much."

"Well. What do you do?" Maddy wasn't wearing gloves, and she blew on her hands to warm them.

"Oh, I don't know. Not anything, I guess. Read. Just regular stuff. Some—sometimes I go sledding. I—I used to, anyway." I sucked my cheeks in and bit down on them.

Maddy smiled at me. "You're funny," she said.

I clamped my mouth shut. I'd said quite enough for one day. Maybe even for life.

"Hey, Caroline." Maddy leaned into me. "Did I say something wrong?"

"No." I had my hands in my pockets. I dug them deeply into my sides.

"Yes, I did. What was it?"

I kept my head down.

"Was it because I said you were funny?"

"I'm not funny."

"Oh, well, I'm sorry. I didn't really mean anything by it. I just meant . . ."

"And anyway, that's not what upsets me," I cut in. "It upsets me that I told you something important and you made a joke about it. 'How about if I say your favorite program is *Hee-Haw*?' You're a real riot, Maddy."

I could see Maddy's mind was clicking back over our conversation. "You mean you were serious about wanting to have your own orchard?"

I stopped walking. "You really want to know what I did in my spare time? Do you really want a good laugh?" My blood must have been traveling a hundred miles an hour. "In my spare time I learned how to grow things."

Maddy just looked at me wide-eyed.

"My Grandpa taught me," I ranted. "He taught me

all about the earth and trees and nature. He taught me to keep strong inside myself. And if that makes me some kind of a freak, then I guess that's exactly what I am!"

"Caroline, I—"

I cut her off. "So if you don't like it, you don't have to hang around me. Nobody's making you. I could be perfectly happy just living all by myself!"

The color drained from Maddy's face as my words slapped against her. "I know that's what you think," she said softly.

"Well, I'll tell you something else, Maddy," I continued. "Some people who grow things are farmers, and other people who grow things are artists, and my grandpa was an artist. So the next time you get a big urge to make one of your farm jokes, why don't you just . . . just . . ."

"Jump in the lake?" Maddy asked. "Stick it in my pipe and smoke it?" She puffed her cheeks out, then smiled.

"I don't care what you do." I felt great. Energized.

"I didn't even realize I'd made any farm jokes. I sure don't feel that way." Maddy touched my arm. "I know how hard it is to—to—well, I can see your grandpa was a special person."

I sniffed and pulled away.

"If you're finished with your speech, then I'd like to tell you something." Maddy's ashen face was pinking up again. "If you think you're the only person in the world who's lost someone close to them or who's had to face change, you're wrong. And I'll tell you something else. If you're going to live your life off somewhere inside yourself, then you'd better not go around with your nose in the air because other people aren't magically sensitive to you. This is the real world, and in the real world you have to learn to speak up."

"My grandpa and I lived in the real world," I defended myself, "and we didn't have to blab every thought we ever had in order to know each other. You don't understand a thing I'm talking about," I accused her.

"I understand a lot more than you realize. And if you'll give me half a chance"—Maddy slipped on a patch of ice and grabbed my arm to steady herself— "I'll throw you down on the sidewalk!" She laughed. Right in the middle of an argument!

"Caroline Warner!" Maddy's voice had softened. "There's more to me than meets the eye. Even yours. Can't we just tell each other when things bother us and then get on with it? Am I supposed to be taking some kind of test or something? Why does it have to be so hard to be friends with you?"

I shrugged my shoulders.

Maddy sighed. "Look. I'm not asking you to marry me. I'm asking you to be my friend! Won't you at least give me a chance?"

I looked up at Maddy. Her eyes were so clear I could see back into them for miles.

"Say yes or I'll write terrible things about you in the school paper."

A smile tugged at the corners of my mouth. "Okay," I heard myself say.

The sidewalks were covered with a thin sheet of ice. "You won't be sorry." Maddy held on to my arm and I didn't pull away as we slipped and slid our way to her house.

"You're really lucky you know what you want to do with your life." Maddy's nose was running from the cold and she sniffed sharply.

"Oh, you mean having an orchard someday?"

"Um-hum. Did you inherit some land or something?"

"No, I think I'd have to lease a few hundred acres at first. Then, when the orchard started making money, I'd be able to buy it. Grandpa Warner left some money in a trust for me that I can have when I turn twenty-one. And the government will make loans, too."

"You have it all figured out, don't you," Maddy said. She drew her collar close and shuddered. "It sure doesn't seem like we have as many options as our parents and grandparents did."

"Yeah," I said, "and it doesn't even seem like our parents have as many options as they *thought* they did.

107

Like, my dad just lost the job I'm sure he counted on having forever. And he should have! Had the job forever, I mean. He does everything so perfectly."

"That's really too bad," Maddy sympathized. "It's pretty scary to think about trying to support myself. I don't know. It's like if you're not a math or computer whiz, you might as well hang it up."

"Tell you what, Maddy," I said. "After my orchard gets going, I'll hire you to do seasonal work. . . ."

Maddy smiled, but the laughter I'd expected didn't follow.

"Well," I asked, "what would you like to do? If— if you could do anything you wanted."

"I *can* do anything I want." Maddy pinched her chin and moved it in two complete circles. "Something with teenagers. Social work, psychology, teaching. Something like that."

A defensive little light bulb went on in my head. "Maddy," I said, "are you out to save me?"

Maddy snorted. "Why would you ask me something like that?"

I didn't answer right away. What I wanted was to make Maddy smile. "I'm sorry I said that." I tapped Maddy's arm. "Okay?"

"Huh?" Maddy said. "Oh. Yeah. That's okay. I was just thinking about what it'd be like to be saved. I think it'd be sort of neat. You know, to have someone delve deep down inside of you and unlock all your secrets. Don't you? I mean, have you ever thought about having yourself analyzed?"

"Oh, sure," I answered quickly. "I've thought about it. But then I figured I was about the *last* person I'd ever want to get to know."

"Caroline!" Maddy laughed. "You're sure one of a kind." She reached over and brushed the snow from the back of my jacket. "And you're about the *first* person I'd ever want to get to know."

10

I'd never seen Maddy's neighborhood up close before. She lived in an older section of town. Many of the houses were seventy-five to a hundred years old. People like the mayor and families of the town founders and business owners lived in them. All the houses were pretty big, and all of them were unique. I liked that. It felt solid.

Maddy's front door was made of shiny oak. When she pushed it open, I could smell pine cleaner and spray wax.

Maddy set her books on a table in the front hall. I

put my books beside hers and started to take off my shoes.

"You don't have to do that," Maddy said. "Let's go get something to drink."

Maddy led the way into the kitchen. There was a woman standing at the sink cleaning vegetables, but Maddy didn't greet her. She opened the refrigerator and took out two cans of Coke.

"Can't we ever get anything besides Coke?" she whined.

The woman at the sink didn't turn around. "What would you like?"

"I don't care. Dr Pepper or Seven-Up or Tab or anything besides Coke!"

Maddy handed a Coke to me. "Let's go up to my room."

"Was . . . was . . . is that your mother?" I whispered, gesturing toward the kitchen.

"No. That's Josie. Our housekeeper."

We walked down the hall past a small room near the stairs. The door to the room was slightly ajar, and I could faintly hear a television set playing.

"You girls be quiet, now," Josie called from the kitchen. "Mrs. Lindsay is resting in the den."

"Oh, that's strange," Maddy said sarcastically.

I followed Maddy up the stairs.

If I lived in her house, I decided, I would sit on the stairs every chance I got. At least at this time of

111

the day. The afternoon sun rested on them and made them dusty and warm. The living room stretched out to the left, and there were windows everywhere. Whole walls made out of windows. It smelled good—like eucalyptus and lemons and old things. On the right I could see a dining room with a patio beyond, and a library with enough books to last a hundred lifetimes. The library looked used. Some of the books were on their sides, some stacked on the floor and a small table. The cushions of the two chairs appeared indented and worn.

"You coming?" Maddy asked.

"Yes. I—I was just looking around," I stammered. "You . . . you sure have a lot of books."

"Uh-huh," Maddy said. "Most of them are pretty boring. I keep a lot of the good ones in my room." Maddy stopped and pushed open a door. "We have arrived! Come on in," she invited me.

Stepping into Maddy's room was like stepping into another world. Well, it certainly wasn't in keeping with the rest of the house, anyway. She had a waterbed with about two dozen stuffed animals strewn across it. There were stacks of records and books all over the place, and posters of people I didn't recognize plastered over an entire wall. Several beat-up cardboard boxes were jammed against her bed.

Maddy looked around the room. "You like it?"

I shook my head. Maddy's room was terrific! "What's

that door over there?" I asked, pointing toward the far side of the room.

"That's the bathroom," Maddy explained. "There's another bedroom on the other side that opens into it, and that'll be Laura's room if, when she comes back home. She, ah, I guess I already told you about Laura." Maddy opened one of the closet doors. "Here. Let me take your coat."

Maddy put both our coats on hangers and pulled some kind of fur coat from the closet. She slipped it on. "This belonged to my mother," she explained. "I use it for a robe."

Maddy walked over to her desk and snapped on a small television set. She flipped the channel from one station to the other, then turned the set off. "There's nothing on anymore," she complained. "What's the matter with you?"

I guess I must have been standing around with my eyes bugged out and my mouth hanging open. "I . . . I . . . doesn't your mother want that coat anymore?"

Maddy glanced down at the coat like it had suddenly appeared out of thin air. "This coat belonged to my real mother. She died," Maddy said dryly. She sat down on the edge of the bed, setting off a chain of ripples within the water mattress.

"Oh. I'm sorry, Maddy. I didn't know."

"It's okay." Maddy pulled the fur coat around her.

"It happened a long time ago. When I was five. A cerebral hemorrhage. Laura was more affected by it than I." Maddy flopped back on the bed, her feet still resting on the floor. "At least I *think* she was more affected than I. Sometimes I wonder how different I'd be if my mother was still alive. And I wonder if any part of me died with her. That probably doesn't make much sense, does it? . . ."

"Yes, it does," I assured her. "It makes perfect sense."

"Anyway," Maddy continued, "not having Laura around has sure been hard. I miss her so much I can't even say it right. You know what I mean?"

"I sure do."

Maddy put her hands behind her head. "I think you'd really like Laura."

I sat cross-legged on the floor by Maddy's feet. "Who's the woman in the den, then?"

"Who? Lynelle? She's my dad's second wife. He married her seven or eight years ago when we were living in Dallas. She had some job in the marketing department at Magnum there, and that's how he met her."

"Do you like her?"

Maddy puffed out her cheeks, then relaxed them. "She's okay, I guess. I liked her a lot more when they first got married. Things—things just haven't worked out the way I expected they would. She was a lot nicer to everybody then. Especially Laura and me. But she, well . . ." Maddy turned over onto her stomach. "She quit her job just before Tyler was born, and—I don't know. Things have just changed. She used to be more caring. A lot more, ah, alive."

I picked at a loose thread in the carpet. "Tyler must be pretty young, then."

"Yeah." Maddy stretched her arms over her head and the silk lining of her coat rustled. "He's four." Maddy rhythmically tapped on the side of the bed with her fingertips.

Maddy turned on her side. "I don't have very many little memories of my mother. You know. Like stuff we did on a daily basis, or things we talked about. But I do have some really strong general memories. She had a ton of books. On all different subjects. She kept them around her in stacks and would have two or three of them going at the same time. Seems pretty ironic, doesn't it?"

"What seems ironic?" It had grown warm in the room, and I pressed the insides of my wrists against the Coke can.

"Just that my mother used her spare time to enrich her life, and Lynelle uses it to waste hers."

I didn't really understand what Maddy was talking about. I switched to another subject. "You're probably going to think I'm really out of it," I confessed, "but who are all those people on the posters?"

Maddy looked at the posters. "Those are all Laura's," she explained. "Hand-me-downs. Most of them are of Jim Morrison and the group he was with. The Doors. Ever heard of them?"

I nodded that I had.

"That one over there is Jimi Hendrix, and the woman in the other ones is Janis Joplin. They were all popular when my mother was young. Laura loved all that music." Maddy pressed her face into her bedspread and sighed. Suddenly she reached over the side of the bed and pulled out a small box from underneath. "This was all stuff I found in Laura's room, too."

The box contained two small plastic bags. What I guessed to be marijuana was in one of them, and the other had a few different colored capsules in it. There was a pair of tweezers with blackened tips tucked along one side.

"That's all drug stuff," I observed.

Maddy sniffed and pushed the box back under the bed. "Yeah. Hand-me-downs." Maddy turned onto her back, and the water in the bed sloshed around. "Remember when I asked you if you took any drugs?"

I wound the thread from Maddy's carpet around my finger. "Yes."

"Well, I'm glad you don't. It seems sort of—I don't know. Insincere."

"Insincere?"

"Well, yeah." Maddy stared straight at the ceiling. I looked up at it, too. "You know what I mean? Those

116

drugs I showed you, all those drugs were part of our parents' generation. We got all their hand-me-downs. We got *their* music, *their* heroes, *their* drugs." Maddy held her arms out like two giant wings. "We got their 'quest for a free spirit,'" she mocked. "About the only things we didn't get were the reasons behind it."

Maddy must have noticed the total blankout on my face.

"You know. The war in Vietnam," she explained. "Abortion. The beginnings of women's rights, racial equality. My mother was really into all that stuff. And she worked for her causes, too. It was different then. There were so many things to think about and be passionate about. It's not like that anymore. Hardly any of the kids I know seem to have a sense of, ah— I don't know. Direction, I guess. Don't you think?"

I shrugged my shoulders.

"Well, just think about it," Maddy said persuasively. "Our parents gave us the best of everything! We have the best schools, the best clothes, the best food, the best parenting, the best environment, the best everything! They worked so hard to give us all the goodies that they left us with nothing to work for on our own! Sometimes don't you just want to rebel?"

"I don't know." I shrugged. "I—I guess I don't really care about things."

Maddy glared at me. "Yes, you do," she insisted.

117

The door to Maddy's room burst open and a rubber snake flew through the air, landing on the bed beside Maddy.

She bounded to the door. "Tyler!" she yelled after the running footsteps. "Haven't you ever heard of knocking? You little brat!" Maddy slammed the door, shutting out his devilish laughter. "Ooh! He is such a hype!" she said to me.

Maddy sat down on the floor and let the coat fall open. Her face was flushed.

"Do you have any brothers or sisters?"

"No. There's just me. Sometimes I wish I did."

Maddy laughed. "And sometimes I wish I didn't!"

Maddy pulled the tab on her can of Coke and put her tongue to the rim where a few drops of the sticky, sweet liquid were spattered. My can remained unopened at my side. In my opinion, Coke is something you drink once a month when you're having popcorn.

Maddy tipped the can to her lips and gulped it. "So," she said, "it's just you and your parents?"

"Um-hum."

"Does your mom work or anything?"

"Yes. She's a buyer at Klugg's."

"Oh!" Maddy clutched the Coke to her heart. "I love that place! Your mom has great taste! I bet you can get a big discount on anything you buy there." Maddy polished off her Coke, then squeezed the empty can.

118

I nodded my confirmation. "I guess. I don't really do a lot of shopping."

"Caroline!" Maddy chided. "That's practically un-American!" Maddy put her hand to her mouth to stifle a hiccup. "Excuse me!"

"Did your mom work?" I asked. Your real mom?"

"No. Not really. During the school year she had a volunteer job twice a week over the lunch hour teaching what they called 'Great Books' to junior high kids. You know. They read and talked about books like *The Red Badge of Courage* and *Treasure Island* and *Moby Dick*. My mother read all those books to Laura and me, too. And, you know, even though they were way over our heads, when I read them now they seem familiar. And I can remember parts!" Maddy pressed her eyelids. "My mother had a really beautiful voice. Sometimes I think I can hear it inside myself."

I ran my hand over the down comforter on Maddy's bed. "Did your mother write poetry, too?"

Maddy was quiet for a moment. "My mother *was* poetry."

Maddy squeaked her index finger around the rim of her soda can, then pitched it toward a wicker basket. It landed cleanly inside with a slight ping. "Two points for the home team!" Maddy sang. "You said your dad lost his job? What did he used to do?"

"He's—he was plant manager at Precision Plastics. But they're tied in with the car industry and just had

119

to close down their Michigan plant. There wasn't enough work being done to support it, I guess."

Maddy stretched out her legs. "Oh, yipes! I hope this doesn't mean you're going to move!"

"No, no," I assured her. "He's just applying for jobs around here. And with my mom working and everything, we're doing okay."

Maddy crossed her outstretched legs at the ankle and stared down at them, calculating, her mouth slightly open.

"What are you thinking about?"

Maddy snapped to attention, as though I'd caught her in the act of snitching a cookie before dinner. "Nothing. Just that I'd like to meet your parents sometime. Your grandma, too. Will you invite me over?" For an instant, her face took on the look of a puppy begging for affection.

"Sure," I said quickly. "You can come over sometime. Tell me more about your sister," I urged her. "Do you have any pictures of her?"

"No. Not, not any recent ones, anyway." Maddy suddenly occupied herself with straightening a wrinkle in her pillow slip.

"How come?" I asked timidly.

"She's changed. She, she's not really herself." Maddy shifted uncomfortably. "But she's getting better."

"Is she sick or something?"

"Yeah. Sort of. Not any horrible disease like cancer

or anything like that. She just kind of got lost along the way."

"What do you mean?"

Maddy's eyes glistened. She blinked and pressed her fingers into her cheeks. "This is really hard for me to talk about," she apologized.

"That's okay," I assured her. "Don't tell me if you don't want."

"No, no. I want to." Maddy took a breath and blew it out, calming herself. "Unless you'd rather not hear it." She smiled.

I lowered my eyes, but only for a second. "I . . . I'd really like to hear it."

"Thanks," Maddy said. "I could use a friend."

"Oh, right!" I snorted.

Maddy looked up at me, puzzled. "You really don't see how alike we are, do you?"

"Oh, Maddy! You have a million friends! What are you talking about?"

"Do you really think having a million friends is possible? You don't let anyone get close," Maddy said, pointing an accusing finger at me. Then she turned the finger to herself. "And I let everyone get close so no one will. We both do the same thing, except you're more obvious."

"I guess I never looked at it that way." There was a gigantic lump in my throat, and I had to swallow. Hard.

"We both do a pretty good job of keeping ourselves a secret, don't we," Maddy said.

I nodded. "Tell me about Laura."

"After my mother died," Maddy started without hesitation, "things went on pretty well. Laura and I were very, very close. Too close, probably. We slept in the same bed and read the same books and were each other's constant playmates. We sort of clung to each other, I guess, but part of the reason was because we had to. Josie never tried to fill in for my mother, and my dad threw himself into his work. He started traveling a lot, and, when he was home, he put in ten- to twelve-hour days six and sometimes seven days a week."

"Maybe he had to," I interrupted. "And Josie, too. Maybe that's the only way they could handle it."

Maddy bit the inside of her cheek. "You could be right," she allowed, "but I really don't want to hear you defend them right now. They did what they had to do, but they sure didn't give a damn about Laura and me."

"How could that be true, Maddy?"

Maddy scowled. "Do you want to hear this or not?"

"Oh. Sorry. I was just trying to help."

Maddy pressed her hands together and flexed them. "A couple of years after my dad and Lynelle got married, Laura changed. And not slowly, either. It was just BAM! I was out of her life. She moved into a room of her own and literally locked me out. She cut all her hair off and pierced one of her ears in thirteen places. She wore tiny ruby studs in twelve of the holes and a huge symbol—kind of like a star—in the bottom one. And she started wearing strange clothes. Sort of like the ones the hippies wore in the sixties. Blousy and gauzy and oversized. And she got so thin! She's my height and she couldn't have weighed more than eighty-five pounds."

"Did she have that anorexa, or whatever it is?" I asked.

"Oh, probably. But that was about the least of my worries. Anorexia of the soul is more like it. It was so horrible, Caroline. She locked herself in her room every night. Sometimes I'd sit in the hall pressed up against her door, and it was really bizarre. I could see flickering lights, like maybe she had candles burning, and there would be long periods of silence followed by moaning and chanting." Maddy shivered.

"Didn't you tell anyone?"

"Sure I did! I told Josie and Lynelle and my dad, but they just said it was a stage she was going through, and that we should try to be patient until she outgrew it. Besides . . . " Maddy sneered. "Lynelle got pregnant, and then Tyler was born, and they were all so wrapped up in him. Laura and I were dispensable."

"Oh, Maddy," I started, but she raised a hand to silence me. "So what finally happened?"

"Well, her grades in school started to slip. She went down in every subject, and even failed a few courses."

"Didn't your dad get concerned then?"

"Oh, sure. He'd talk to her and she'd promise to try harder, but it just got worse. And then she started pretending she was sick so she wouldn't have to go to school. Toward the end, like the last week she was with us, she just locked herself in her room and refused to come out for anything. My dad was away on business at the time, so Lynelle called him and he came home. It took all that to get his attention. What a nightmare."

"So then what happened?" I encouraged her.

"I don't really know. Dad made me go to my room and close the door. I kept a pillow over my head, but I could still hear them."

My mind raced back to the time I'd spent with a pillow over my head while Grandpa Warner's orchard fell. I blinked back tears.

"Dad started out knocking on her door and calling her name, but she didn't answer. Finally, he broke the door down." Maddy put her hands over her ears. "I can still hear the wood splitting."

I closed my eyes and nodded knowingly. "What happened then?" I asked numbly.

"She—she—my dad brought her to the hospital. She didn't slash her wrists or overdose or anything like that. She just sort of willed herself away. I don't know. I didn't understand. I still don't. He—my dad—didn't know what else to do with her, I guess. Laura was in the hospital for a few days, a regular hospital, and from there she went to, you know, the loony bin." Maddy laughed suddenly.

"Is she still there? In the hospital, I mean?"

"No. She was in the hospital quite a long time, though. Six or seven months. Now she's living in a group home and going to a special school."

There was a loud bang on the door, as though something had been hurtled against it.

"Isn't Tyler just charming?" Maddy asked. "Knock it off, Ty."

"Knock it off, Ty," the voice on the other side of the door mimicked.

Maddy rolled her eyes. "Let's just ignore him." Tyler's interruption had given Maddy time to compose herself. She patted my shoulder and smiled. "Did I tell you Laura might be coming home for Christmas?"

"Yeah, you did."

"She really is a lot better. She's not taking any drugs now. Dad says that if everything goes well when she's home, he'll consider letting her spend the summer here."

"That'd be great. I hope I'll get to meet her."

"Oh, you will," Maddy promised. Tyler's door banging began anew. "Hey!" Maddy yelled. "Do you ever go to the football games?"

"No. Not really," I said loudly. The banging stopped just as I'd said "really," and Maddy and I both laughed as the word bounced off the walls. Our laughter was all Tyler needed. He pounded fiercely.

"Well, I want you to come to the game with me a week from tomorrow, and then I'm having a party after." Maddy put her hands over her ears to block out the hammering on the door.

"Well, I don't know. Who all's coming?" I shouted.

"Just . . . Tyler! Will you please stop that? Just a few kids from school. I hope anyway. Maybe nobody will show up when they find out my parents are going to be here."

"Maybe. I don't know."

"You'll come," Maddy decided. She got up and raced to the door. When she opened it, Tyler fell into the room.

"Tyler! What are you doing!"

He picked himself up and gave Maddy a little shove. "Well, you told me I should knock," he said, tapping Maddy in the ribs with his fists.

She pushed his hands away. "What do you want?"

"Josie says somebody's here. She says Caroline Baroline Daroline has to go home." Tyler turned to me and stuck his tongue out. "Last one down is a rotten poop!"

I got up from the floor. "That must be my mom.

She said she'd stop by after work to pick me up. I'd better be going."

Maddy stood with a hand on each side of the door frame. "Oh. I wish you could stay longer. . . ."

"Well, we can get together again," I said. "Maybe— maybe you can come to my house sometime."

Maddy brightened. "How about Saturday?"

"Well." I hesitated. "I don't know. I'll have to check. Maybe."

Maddy removed her hands from the door. "You want me to walk you down?"

A car horn sounded impatiently from the driveway. "No. That's okay. I'd better hurry."

"See you in school tomorrow," Maddy said. It felt almost like a threat.

"Okay. . . . Well, ah, thanks for the Coke. And for having me over. 'Bye!"

"Bye-bye!"

I rushed down the stairs as quietly as I could, not wishing to attract any attention.

I was filled to the brim.

11

"Did you plant all these?" Maddy knelt and touched one of the dead, brown marigolds that had grown so heartily along our fence all summer.

"No. You don't have to plant them. You just do a special little marigold dance," I teased her.

"Okay." Maddy laughed. "So I'm a city slicker."

Josie had delivered Maddy to my house at eleven o'clock on Saturday morning. She'd met my parents, and we'd all had lunch together. We were now, at Maddy's insistence, on our way to Grandma's house.

128

Torn is the only word that comes to mind when I try to describe how I felt about Maddy's arrival in my tidy world. Sometimes I feel like two people: the one who lives so peacefully inside me, and the one who has to face life on earth. And it seems the part of me who lives in the world has to spend most of her time guarding the part who lives inside. The thought of having Maddy for a friend was intriguing. Even exciting. But, still, it would take some time to make a place for her without messing everything up.

"I really love your parents, Caroline," Maddy chatted. "And your house is wonderful. A real home. I don't know. There's such a solid feel to it." Maddy kicked a stone as we walked along. "And I can't believe your dad makes all your own bread. I'd probably weigh about five thousand pounds if I lived here." Maddy caught her stone on a wrong angle and it skidded off the roadway into a ditch. "Ooh! I can't wait to meet your Grandma!"

"She's pretty old, Maddy. Eighty-five! And she's also pretty set in her ways," I warned. "I—I hope you . . . well, I hope you like her and are tolerant if— if she—"

"Hey! What is this?" Maddy interrupted. "A lesson in how to be kind to old people? Well, thanks a whole lot, Caroline, but I really don't need it. I have grandparents of my own, you know."

"No! No. I'm sorry. It's just that sometimes she's a little cranky, and I didn't want you to take it personally."

"I won't," Maddy said icily. "Hey! Is that her dog? What kind is he?"

"Uh-huh. We don't really know. We think he's part collie and part beagle. Hi, Bill!" I greeted him.

Old Bill had his ears down and teeth bared. He growled as we approached.

"It's okay, Billy Boy," I called. "Nobody's going to hurt you." Not positively sure how Old Bill would react to Maddy, I kept her out of Old Bill's reach and hurried her into the house.

"Watch your step, Maddy. These steps aren't all that sturdy."

Grandma was in the kitchen, and she had a very docile smile. Oh-oh. That meant she was off in her own world.

"Hi, Grandma!" I held the door open and ushered Maddy into the house.

"Hello, Georgia," Grandma said to me.

Often when Grandma is in a foggy state of mind, she confuses me with my mother.

"No, Grandma. It's me. Caroline." I took Maddy by the arm and pushed her into the foreground. "And this is my friend, Madelyn."

"Why, heavens no!" Grandma exclaimed. "I'm not mad at Lynn! Any friend of yours is a friend of mine."

130

Maddy and I exchanged smiles. "No, Grandma. This is Madelyn Lindsay!" I said loudly.

"Well. How about that. You come right in, Lynn. You girls go ahead and set yourselves down at the table. I just got to finish feeding the ants."

Grandma had two pieces of dried bread in her hands. She rubbed some crumbs off into a neat little pile on the countertop. I glanced around and saw half a dozen similar piles. "Why are you doing that, Grandma?"

"Yes, it is," she answered sweetly.

"Grandma!" I shouted, my stomach tightening. "Why are you feeding the ants?"

She turned to face me, astonished. "Because they're all God's creatures!" she explained. "But don't you girls worry. There'll be plenty left over for you."

I looked quickly at Maddy. She was watching Grandma, a tender expression softening her face. I took a deep breath and began to relax.

"Here you go, girls," Grandma said. She placed what was left of the bread in front of us. "Would you like some nice jam to put on that?"

"We've already had lunch—" I started.

"I would!" Maddy interrupted.

Grandma patted the top of Maddy's head. "You're a good girl, Lynn."

The old woman sat down at the table, forgetting her offer of jam. "Yep," she said, flattening her hands on the tabletop, "I've got forty-seven of them now."

"Forty-seven what, Grandma?" Although I was the one who'd asked, Grandma looked at Madelyn to answer.

"Ants! I started out with only two, three of the little rascals, and now this morning I counted forty-seven. It's getting harder and harder to keep 'em all straight!"

"Oh, I'll bet it is!" Maddy agreed in a clear voice. "That must be a lot of work for you!"

"Yep," Grandma said proudly. "Yes, it is. But I don't mind. Not at all. No, sir. I never have had a lazy bone in my body." Grandma straightened her back. "Of course, they never set still, so it could be I was counting some of them more than once." She laughed.

Maddy nudged me with her foot and winked.

"Grandpa will be back any minute now. He had to check on the water lines that run into the apple shed. They froze up on us last year. You remember that, Georgia? What time is it, anyway?" Grandma craned her neck in order to see the clock on the stove. "Two o'clock already? Well, he should be right back. He promised to take me out motoring today."

"Grandma," I said, "I don't think . . ."

"Where are you going?" Maddy asked.

"We thought we'd take a ride out to Stevensville. They got that cider press out there, and homemade doughnuts! You ever been out that way, Lynn?"

132

Maddy put a hand to her brow. "No. I never have. I've heard about it, though."

Grandma's forehead wrinkled. "Heard about what?" she demanded harshly.

"A—about the cider press."

"So!" Grandma snapped. "Who hasn't?"

I pushed my chair back from the table and stood behind Grandma. "Want me to brush your hair?"

"What you trying to tell me, girl? That my hair's a mess?"

"No. No. Not at all. Your hair is beautiful. I just thought you might like to have it brushed."

"When trouble comes knocking, you don't have to let him in," she declared. "And a stitch in time saves nine, so if you've got any fancy ideas, you can just lead them to water." She tilted her head back to look at me. "But you can't make them drink."

Maddy covered her mouth with a paper napkin to hide a smile.

"Then Grandpa and I thought we'd stop in at The Three Sisters'. That's the only place you can grind your own coffee beans. Grandpa can't tolerate that stuff you buy already ground up and sealed in a tin can."

"Who are the three sisters?" Maddy asked.

"It's not really a 'who,'" I explained, "it's more of a 'what.' Three Sisters' is a grocery store."

Actually, The Three Sisters' Store had been out of business for years. I don't even think the building is standing anymore, and the women who owned it are long gone.

"The three sisters is Edith, Enid, and Edna Ver Sloot." Grandma had three fingers extended on her right hand, and she flexed them several times. "Wait, now. Come to think of it, I believe Enid passed on a few years back." Grandma folded one finger under. "Not a one of them girls ever married," Grandma said, "and if you ever seen them, you wouldn't have to ask why. Every single one of them, ugly as sin. They all have kind of a horsey look about them. Great big women they are. Great big heads. Big jaws. And meaner than the dickens! All three of them. They have themselves an apartment up there above the store, and there's always some kind of infernal bickering going on. Never will understand how it is they've managed to live together and work together all these years. The Three Sisters' Store. Even though Enid died, they still call it that. And they still include Enid in their arguments—'Enid would have said this. Enid would have done that.' And on and on and on. Wretched women. Just wretched. But they got that good coffee."

"Why don't I get the picture album out, Grandma, and then you can tell Mad—er—Lynn all about our family."

Without waiting for an answer, I hurried to the parlor bedroom and pulled the photo album out from underneath the bed. Sometimes getting Grandma to talk about the past helps her to get a better grip on the present.

When I returned to the kitchen, Maddy and Grandma were leaning toward each other, obviously enjoying each other's company. I slid between them, placed the album on the table, and opened it. "Look, Grandma! Here's me on my two, three, four, five, six," I said, counting the candles on the cake, "sixth birthday!"

Maddy moved in closer. "Oh, Caroline! What a little doll! Your hair was so long!"

"So long," Grandma said sadly, reaching for Maddy's hand. "I'm glad you could stop over."

"Grandma, we're not—"

Maddy's voice overrode mine. "Would you like us to stay a little longer?"

Grandma patted Maddy's hand. "Yes. I'd like that very much."

Grandma pulled the album closer to her and began slowly turning the pages, pausing occasionally to tenderly run her withered hand over some of the pictures. She kept licking her lips and making a little clicking sound with her jaw. Maddy and I waited reverently as Grandma journeyed back. Suddenly tears sprang to the old woman's eyes.

"What are you thinking about, Grandma?" I asked softly.

She stared straight forward, rapidly blinking back tears. "I was thinking about Mama. Oooh," she mourned, "bless her little soul."

"Could, could, why don't you tell us about her," I gently persuaded her.

Grandma studied Maddy's face, her grief disappearing as quickly as it had come. "Have I ever told you about Mama?" she asked calmly.

"No," Maddy said. "But it would really make me happy if you would."

"Well," Grandma said, leaning back in her chair and taking on her storyteller voice, "Mama was born in Germany in a little town near Munich. . . ."

"That's where my sister Laura was born!" Maddy exclaimed.

Grandma ignored her comment. When she's relating a story, she gets very single-minded and won't acknowledge anyone else's thoughts.

". . . and right after she was married, Mama and her new husband decided to sell all their belongings and scrape together all the money they could so they could move to the United States. Of course, that was a much bigger deal back then than it would be nowadays." Grandma tapped her fingers on the tabletop.

"When was that?" Maddy asked.

"Oh, right after they were married."

"Yes, I know. But what year?"

"Let's see." Grandma thought. "Must have been the late 1890's. They came over on a ship. A freighter. When they got to America, all they had was eighteen dollars and each other. They didn't know a soul here, but they found out about a Dutch settlement in Michigan, so that's where they decided to go. I guess they thought Dutch and German was close enough. They built themselves a little cabin not too far from here. I think it got tore down in about 1940. You remember that, Georgia?"

I shook my head yes.

"Well, good," Grandma said sternly. "Now don't interrupt me no more."

Maddy chuckled.

"I won't," I promised.

"Yes, sir," Grandma continued, "they built themselves a cabin and cleared some land in hopes of starting a farm. But they wasn't here more than three months when Mama's husband got sick and died. Diphtheria. That left Mama a new bride all alone in a strange country where she couldn't even speak the language." Grandma paused, her eyes misting over. Maddy shifted uncomfortably.

"But that didn't stop Mama's dream," Grandma went on, composing herself. "When news of her husband's death reached Germany, Mama's parents—she was from a wealthy family—sent Mama money with instructions to return home. But not Mama. She sent the money back with a note that said, 'I am staying.' She was sixteen years old at the time. And she was pregnant."

"Wow." Maddy loudly sighed. "And here I thought the Women's Movement started with *my* mother's generation."

"She done all right for herself, too. She let herself out as a day worker. Doing laundry, scrubbing floors, cooking, sewing. She done whatever she had to do. Then, after I was born, she took me right along with her."

"Did she ever remarry?" Maddy asked, intrigued by the old woman's story.

"Yes, she did. She met a carpenter named John who went to her church. He lived about ten miles from here, and he'd come courting twice a week. He'd come by horse and buggy every Friday night. Then, after church on Sundays, he'd stay and take supper with us. I was five years old when they got married. The picture is as clear as can be in my mind. Why is it, Georgia," Grandma said, turning her attention to me, "that I can remember things that happened years and years ago, but I can't remember what I had for breakfast this morning?"

I shrugged my shoulders. "I don't know, Grandma."

"Anyway, Mama made me a dress for the wedding out of white organdy and lace. And when I walked into the church that day, pretty as a picture, your Grandpa Warner, who was six at the time, turned to his mother and said, 'There's my girl, Ma.' And that was that. I been his girl ever since."

"Did your mother ever get to see her parents again?" Maddy asked.

"No. Her parents were too stubborn to come here, and Mama never had enough money to go there. They wrote letters back and forth, though." Grandma closed the photo album and her eyes clouded. "Mama used to tell me all about her parents. But then one day a letter come from her uncle back in Germany. Mama must've known there was something wrong— she had a sense about those things—because she took the letter into that little pantry we had off the kitchen. She stayed in there for fifteen, twenty minutes, and I could hear her crying. When she finally came out, she took me on her lap in the rocking chair and said, 'Your grandpa and grandma died.' She rocked me all afternoon, and, from that day on, Mama never mentioned either one of them again."

Grandma pressed her lips together and closed her eyes in a signal to us that her story was over. Maddy didn't catch it.

"Tell us some more about what it was like when you were growing up," she coaxed her.

"No, no, no, girl. Memories is just like anything else. If you go using them too much they get all wore out."

139

Maddy folded her hands and stared down at them, smiling. "Thank you for sharing some of your memories with me."

Grandma stiffened. "I'm awful tired now. Why don't you girls scoot along home."

I was the first to rise. I gave Grandma a hug and kissed her cheek. "I'll be over again tomorrow, Grandma."

"Good-bye, Caroline. You bring that Lynn girl back here again. I like her."

Maddy put her arms around my grandma. " 'Bye, Grandma," she said. "I'm so glad I got to meet you."

The hair on the back of my neck stood on end to hear Maddy call her "Grandma."

"You come back and see me again real soon! Caroline! Don't forget to bring that Lynn girl back!" Grandma called.

Well, at least Grandma remembered who I was.

Once outside the house, Maddy turned to me. "Oh, Caroline, do you know how lucky you are? To have your grandmother living so close?"

"Yes," I answered coolly.

Maddy drew her arms up to her sides and began jogging in place. "I am so full of energy! Race you back to your house!" With that, she was off.

I stood and watched. When she was thirty paces up the road, she stopped and called back, "Well! Are you coming or not?"

I knelt to tie my shoe. "Not," I muttered.

Maddy cupped her hand to her ear. "What? I couldn't hear you!"

"I'm coming!" I said sharply. "My shoelace was untied."

I could see Maddy's surprise at the harshness of my retort. She brushed her hair back with one hand. "Sorry," she said.

12

"Why are you avoiding me?"

Someone bumped my arm, and I moved out of the way so my classmates could get through the door.

"I'm *not* avoiding you. I've just been really busy."

Maddy wasn't about to buy my story. "Come on, Caroline, I'm not that dense. What is it? Didn't your parents approve of me or something?"

"Of course they approve of you," I said.

Approve of her! My parents were crazy about Maddy. In fact, they talked about her darling personality and how pretty she was and how polite she was, et cetera, et cetera, et cetera, all week. And every time I went to Grandma's, she asked about "that Lynn girl," too. They practically all came right out and told me they wished I could be more like wonderful, marvelous Madelyn.

"Walk home with me," Maddy urged. "Let's talk about whatever it is that's bothering—"

"Nothing is bothering me!" I interrupted. "And I can't walk home with you. I have to go see Mr. Daverman."

"About what?" Maddy asked.

"*I* don't know!" Maddy's prying was starting to get on my nerves. "He just asked me to stop in after school today because he wanted to talk to me about something."

"Hmm," Maddy said. "I wonder what that could be."

"Look, Maddy. I've got to go."

Maddy leaned so close I could feel the moisture in her breath. "I'll walk with you to Mr. Daverman's room and wait outside until you're through with your talk. Then we can go back to my house."

"Sorry. I can't today. I have to get right home." I pushed past Maddy and started down the hall, my ears straining to hear if she was following me. She wasn't. Maybe she'd gotten the hint. There was no place for Maddy in my life.

The door to Mr. Daverman's room was partially

closed. When I tapped on it, it opened a little wider.

"Yes?" Mr. Daverman asked.

"It's Caroline Warner."

A chair scraped across the tile floor. "Come on in, Caroline," Mr. Daverman called.

David Kettering was seated in front of Mr. Daverman's desk. He smiled as I entered the room. "Hi, Caroline."

"Hi," I said to them both.

Mr. Daverman motioned to the chair next to David. "Have a seat, Caroline. You and David know each other?"

David stretched and then clasped his hands behind his neck. "Oh, sure. Caroline and I go way back."

David and I had gone to the same grade school. He was my first great love. Come to think of it, he was my only great love. Anyway, we'd played together at recess and sometimes after school until we were about in third grade and the teasing became too much to bear.

David is pretty popular, in a quiet sort of way. He's student editor of the school paper. Although we hardly ever say anything more than "Hi" and "How are you?" anymore, I still feel a special bond with him. I'm sure he doesn't feel it, though.

David and I had kissed each other once. In the coatroom in first grade. The memory of it made my face burn.

144

David rose from his chair. "Well," he said to Mr. Daverman, "I want to get these edited before you see them, so I'll drop them off sometime tomorrow."

"Thanks for stopping by," Mr. Daverman said.

"Thank you!" David touched my shoulder. "Good seeing you, Caroline."

I just *knew* my face was red. "Good . . . good—it was nice seeing you, too," I stammered.

"Oh, by the way," David asked, "are you going to Maddy's party after the game tomorrow?"

"Um, I—I'm not sure," I mumbled.

"Maddy told me you were going to be there. I hope you come. I think it'll be a lot of fun. See you all later!"

After David left, Mr. Daverman got up and sat directly in front of me on the edge of his desk. He was wearing a pale blue sweater that emphasized the blue in his eyes. "I wanted to tell you how very much I enjoy having you as a student. I always look forward to seeing your work. And you've never disappointed me!"

I stiffened my body so I wouldn't squirm. "Thank you. I really like being in your class."

Mr. Daverman crossed his feet at the ankles and leaned back on his hands. "Would you consider a position on the school paper?"

"I—I— Well, I'm really not that kind of writer."

"What kind is that?" Mr. Daverman took a roll of Certs from his pocket and offered me one.

I was going to say no thanks, but then realized he might be offering me a Cert because I had bad breath. I took one. "Thanks," I said, putting the mint in my mouth. "Well, I do okay writing poetry and stuff like that, but I'm not very good at writing about real things that happen. You know. Like reporting things."

"Actually," Mr. Daverman said, "what the staff has in mind is starting a poetry corner."

"You mean you want to put my poems in the school paper?"

"Well, yes. Yours and some of the other students'. I've seen some dynamite poetry so far this year. What we'd really like is for you to be the editor of that section."

"Me? Why?"

"For a couple of reasons." Mr. Daverman crunched his Cert. "First, because you've written some outstanding poetry and second, because you seem to have a special sensitivity to what being a young adult is all about." He finished chewing his mint and swallowed. "When we discussed doing a poetry corner, your name came up, and, after reading some of the things you've done for this class, the staff voted unanimously to ask you to be the poetry editor."

Maddy! She was at it again! It had to be one of her big ideas. You give some people an inch and they practically move in. My hands clenched so tightly my nails dug deeply into them. "No," I said. "I, I'm not really qualified to do that."

"Sure you are!" Mr. Daverman encouraged me. "You're a natural! Everything you've written for class is so typical—in a unique way, of course—of the way people your age feel. And I'd be willing to give you all the help you need."

Typical! I shudder every time I hear the word! "No. No. I don't think so."

Mr. Daverman uncrossed his legs. "I'll tell you what. Don't give me an answer right now. Let's see. Today is Thursday. Why don't you think it over and let me know on Monday?"

I stood abruptly and turned from Mr. Daverman. "Okay," I agreed. "I'll let you know. Thanks, ah, thank you for asking me."

"I hope you change your mind. You have a talent that deserves sharing."

"Thank you," I said, hurrying toward the door. "I'll—I'll let you know. On Monday."

"See you in class tomorrow," Mr. Daverman said.

"Okay. 'Bye. And thanks."

I knew the bus had already left, and a shiver ran through me as I anticipated the walk home. Maybe I'd run. I'm sure I could have reached speeds of five hundred miles an hour, I was so pumped up over Maddy's maneuvering.

147

The wind whipped up under my coat as I half ran, half walked down the street. Within minutes my legs were numbed from the cold. I kept my head down and collar up and didn't even hear the car approach until its horn sounded.

It was Mother.

She leaned over and opened the door on the passenger side. "Hey, good-lookin'! Like a ride?"

The car heater roared and blasted hot air on my legs as I slid into the car. "You're a real riot, Mom. Where you going this time of day?"

"Dad called," she shouted over the din. "He asked if I could sneak out a little early today. He said he has an announcement!"

"Oh!" I gasped. "Do you think he got a job? Did he have any interviews today?"

The windshield was fogging up. "Stop breathing, will you?" She ran a gloved hand over the glass to clear her field of vision, then switched on the defroster. "Not that I know of, but it sure sounds promising!"

The radio was playing softly. When Mom heard the words, "special weather bulletin," she put her hand up for silence and raised the volume on the radio.

"This is meteorologist Clay Larson reporting for WZMI radio news. There's a low pressure ridge situated just to the southwest of us moving northeasterly at a rapid rate. We expect the outer edge of the

148

low to reach the Michigan shoreline within the hour," the announcer blared. "This storm is producing ten- to twelve-foot waves on Lake Michigan and wind gusts of up to sixty-five miles per hour. Chicago has already had eight inches of snow, and, I'm sorry to say, it looks like the storm will continue to grow in intensity before reaching us. There is a traveler's advisory in effect for all of western Michigan. All motorists are advised to get off the roads as soon as possible. Keep your radios tuned to station WZMI for further weather updates. This is Clay Larson repeating, a winter storm producing blizzard conditions is expected to reach our area by five o'clock this afternoon. All motorists are urged . . ."

Mother lowered the volume. "Oh!" she squealed. "I love extremes!"

When we pulled into our driveway I noticed a few roof shingles rising and falling with the wind. "Oh-oh," I said, "looks like we're going to lose half our roof!"

Mother backed the car up to get a better look. "You're right! Well, half the roof is an exaggeration, but it does look like we might lose some shingles."

Mom and I braced ourselves for the short walk from the garage to the back door. We were practically blown into the house, and a gust of wind slammed the door shut behind us.

Suddenly Dad stepped out from around the corner

149

with clarinet in hand. He brought the instrument to his lips and played the first few bars of "Happy Days Are Here Again."

"Richard!" Mother yelped. "You scared me half to death!"

"Only half?" he complained. "And here I thought I could keep all my earnings for myself."

Dad was wearing his very best suit. The collar on his white shirt was starched so stiffly it looked as though it would crack in two with the slightest pressure.

"How come you're so dressed up, Dad?"

"Oh," he said matter-of-factly, "I had a little job interview today."

"Where?" Mom asked.

Dad hooked his thumbs in his pants pockets. "My dear wife and devoted daughter. You are in the presence of the new plant manager of the toys division of Magnum International. Please take your place in line to kiss my ring."

"You are kidding me!" Mother exclaimed. "How'd you hear about the job opening? Why didn't you tell me?"

"You have your darling daughter to thank for that," Dad said.

I was so stunned that Dad would even consider taking a job at Magnum International, I couldn't react.

"Well! What happened? Tell me!" Mother urged him.

"I got a phone call this morning from Albert Lindsay's secretary asking me if it would be possible to meet with him this afternoon at two o'clock for an interview. It seems they've grown so much the present plant manager felt he had to give up half the operation, and they needed someone with managerial experience and someone who could start immediately to take over the other half. And that's where Caroline comes in. She's spent some time bragging on her old pa to Maddy—that's Mr. Lindsay's daughter—and when Mr. Lindsay mentioned the problem at the plant over dinner, Maddy told him about me!"

Mother threw her arms around him. "Yahooey!" she sang. "I *knew* something terrific would come along! I just *knew* it! When do you start?"

"Monday morning." Dad looked in my direction. "Well," he said, "are you just going to stand there with your mouth hanging open, or are you going to congratulate me?"

"Congratulations," I answered automatically. "I, I'm really happy for you."

"Well, come here!" Dad was so excited he didn't notice my distress. "I have a great big hug saved up just for you. And I have one for Maddy, too!"

I kept my arms crossed over my chest as Dad hugged me.

The windows of the house rattled as the first of the storm reached us.

"Did you hear about the blizzard we're supposed to get?" Mom asked.

"Yes!" Dad answered. "Sounds like it's going to be a dandy!"

"I—I think I'll go check on Grandma before we eat dinner. I want to see if she needs anything and to make sure she lets Old Bill in for the night."

"That's a good idea, Caroline," Dad said. "I was going to take you all out for dinner tonight, but maybe it'd be better if we just stayed in. How about if I make pizza? Would that be festive enough?"

"That's great," I said, failing to generate as much enthusiasm as I'd hoped. "I won't be gone long."

The air was so frigid as I fought my way through the bone-chilling gusts that each breath froze up at the base of my throat. I was light-headed by the time I reached Grandma's yard.

Old Bill was huddled up inside his dog house. He rose to greet me and gave his tail a quick flip.

"I love you, Bill." I knelt and wrapped my arms around the raggedy scruff on his neck. "You want to go in the house, Boy?"

Old Bill pressed against me, shivering. There were tiny little icicles of frozen drool around his muzzle. With my gloved hand I wiped them away and kissed the star in the middle of his forehead.

A small, flat piece of an old bone stuck out of the snow. I grasped it, smoothed a writing surface, and wrote my name. It looked out of place, and I patted the snow to erase it.

"You're all I've got, Old Bill."

My mother's bent on getting all the gusto she can out of life; my grandmother's lost to herself; my father's gone over to the enemy camp; and my friend would just as soon wear me as a trinket on her already overloaded charm bracelet.

The single light of a jetliner flying below the clouds plodded across the darkened sky. There were probably a hundred people sitting in that dot. All being hurtled from one place to the next. Crazy. Just crazy. It made me feel small.

Grandpa used to shake his head in disgust whenever planes trespassed across his sky. As I watched the light disappear over the horizon I pretended it was a falling star.

13

It stormed all night.

I was on the verge of wakefulness all through the storm, some small part of my consciousness tuned in and absorbing its fury. At times I could feel the powerful winds coming right through the walls and I burrowed deeply into my blankets and pillows. Snug and safe. Like a cocoon.

The wind blasted with such force that all the windows on the south side of the house were packed over with snow. First reports of the snowfall indicated we'd received eighteen inches, with drifts of five to seven feet.

Emergency road crews had been out since four in the morning, their red and yellow lights coloring the crystal white canvas. The roads this far out of town had quickly blown shut after the plows left and were once again impassable. Our phone lines were down, although we still had water and electricity. School and all school activities had been canceled, and most businesses were going to delay opening, if they opened at all.

As soon as I awoke, I bundled myself in layers of clothing and started for Grandma's.

I felt as though I were in a dream. The wind was still whipping, but the snow was so deep and angled that it never quite reached the ground. It was like walking in a vacuum. I sank well past my knees with each step, but the snow was dry and light and powdery, so walking wasn't too difficult.

Except for the wind above, there wasn't a sound. It reminded me of the way things were during my childhood—no cars and trucks passing by; no people rushing off to here and there and wherever they rush to; Mother waiting at home.

I had to shovel away a few feet of snow drifted against Grandma's door before I could pull it open. As soon as I did, Old Bill barreled out, furiously circled round and round a tree in a vain attempt to pack the snow, then lifted his leg. A cloud of steam rolled over him. He sniffed around a bit, then wandered back to me, panting.

"Feel better?" I laughed.

Old Bill pushed ahead of me and ran into the kitchen.

The aroma of apples and cinnamon made my mouth water. Grandma was just taking a loaf pan from the oven.

"Hi, Grandma! Whatcha making?"

She turned the soggy contents out onto a bread board. "Banana bread."

"Oh. It smells like apple," I observed.

"Well, I should hope so," Grandma scolded me. "What did you expect apple bread to smell like?"

"How'd you like that storm?" I asked. It was pretty obvious a change of subject was in order.

"Of *course* I didn't buy it in a store! You know I never touch that stuff! Set yourself down and I'll cut you a piece."

My feet bumped up against Old Bill underneath the table. Grandma set a plate in front of me with a glob of "apple bread" on it. "How'd you make this, Grandma?"

"Oh. With a little bit of this and a little bit of that."

Grandma always did take pleasure in having secret recipes. But from the looks of the offering in front of me, this was one recipe the world wasn't going to beat down her door to get. I scooped some up with two fingers, and, when Grandma wasn't looking, put my hand underneath the table. Old Bill's warm tongue eagerly lapped it.

Grandma filled the sink with sudsy water.

"Aren't you going to have any, Grandma?"

"No. I only like to make it. Not eat it. That don't hold no joy for me."

"Well, then, could I take it home? Mother and Dad would really enjoy it, too."

Grandma smiled proudly. "Why, yes. I'll wrap it up for you."

I held another glob under the table. Old Bill sniffed it but wouldn't take it. I reached for a paper napkin to wipe my fingers off, then nudged Old Bill with my foot. "Thanks a lot, pal . . ." I whispered.

"It's under the sink," Grandma said, "where I always keep it."

"What's under the sink?"

"The pail!" Grandma snapped. "You couldn't have wanted it all that badly if you can't even remember what you asked me for."

"No," I agreed. "I guess not."

"Why don't you go along home now. And take that dog with you. He spent the whole night sniffing under my bed. I don't think I got more than two hours' sleep, what with the wind howling and the dog sniffing."

I walked over and stood beside her at the sink. "You

do look tired, Grandma. Why don't you go back to bed?"

"Don't tell me what to do, girl." Grandma plunged the crusty loaf pan into the sink. "I had a whole lifetime of that already."

I slid the apple bread, board and all, into a grocery sack. "Thank you for the bread, Grandma."

"You're entirely welcome," she said, her disposition softening. "You come back and see me tomorrow."

"I will," I promised, kissing her cheek. "Come on, Bill!"

Old Bill and I followed a snowplow all the way back to my house. Snow shot out of the side along the road, piling huge banks of snow. I threw some snowballs to Old Bill and he scurried after them and ate them. The plow turned down our street.

Mother and Dad were outside and had just finished shoveling the driveway. As the plow passed by it deposited several feet of snow at the base of our drive. Dad shook his shovel at the driver, and I could see the driver shrug.

"Ha, ha!" I teased.

Dad wasn't in the mood to be humored. "It's pretty funny, all right," he grumbled. "So funny, in fact, that you can take your mother's place and help me shovel it out again."

"Oh, good." Mother shivered. "I'm just about frozen! What's he doing here?"

Old Bill had just appeared from around a snowbank and ran merrily to greet them.

"Grandma didn't want him in the house," I explained. "He did too much sniffing around last night. And I really think it's too cold for him to be outside."

"You're probably right." Dad removed his gloves and beat them against his hips to shake the snow off. "What's in the bag?"

"A present from Grandma!" I opened the bag and Dad peeked in.

"What is this?"

"It's apple bread!" I snapped, imitating Grandma's voice. "What'd you think?"

Dad grinned. He pinched off a small amount and put it on his tongue. "Ach! That's disgusting! She must have put a cup of salt in there!"

Mother handed her shovel to me. "Here. Give the bread to me and I'll get rid of it." She took the bag and walked toward the house with Old Bill at her heels. She gestured toward a small pile of roof shingles they had uncovered as they shoveled. "Isn't that wonderful?" she asked.

"Terrific," I answered.

Dad slipped his gloves back on, then laid a hand beside my nose, giving it a little nudge. He studied my face. "There," he decided. "That's better."

"What are you doing?" I asked.

"Oh, just straightening your nose. It seemed to be a little out of joint last night."

I rubbed my nose and slid the shovel underneath a pile of weightless snow.

"I really think we should talk about it," Dad persisted. "It's pretty obvious you're not that thrilled with my new job."

"Well, I just . . . Well. Do you really *want* to work for Magnum?"

"Sure I do. Why wouldn't I?"

"Well, it just seems a little arranged," I said.

"What do you mean by that?"

"I don't know. It just seems like a dumb way to get a job. I mean by your daughter telling her girl friend about you, and then her telling her dad."

"Thanks for the vote of confidence, Caroline." Snow stuck to Dad's shovel and he banged on the back of it. "Maybe your friendship with Maddy did give me an in I wouldn't have otherwise had, but Mr. Lindsay is a smart man and he would not have offered me the job as a favor. I have the right background and track record to qualify for the job."

"I . . . I know," I said, embarrassed. A gust of wind blew some snow into my face. I deserved it. "Is . . . is working at Magnum what you really *want* to do?" I asked timidly.

"It will be challenging, I think," Dad answered. "And the pay and benefits are better than my old job. More responsibility, too. The rewards are certainly greater than the ones you get for being unemployed. And I don't just mean financially."

"But is that really what you want to do?"

"What I really want?" Dad leaned against his shovel. "No, actually. What I really want to do is play clarinet in a jazz band. That's what I've always wanted to do."

"Well, did you ever try it?" I pressed my gloved hands against my frozen cheeks.

"I was in a few different groups when I was in college." Dad gave up on trying to lift the powdery snow and used his shovel like a plow to push it aside instead. "And, right after Mother and I found out we were pregnant for you, I had the chance to join a band that was really quite established. In Chicago."

"Why didn't you do it?" The snowplow had turned around to clear the other side of the road, and I had to raise my voice and ask the question again.

"Because!" Dad shouted. "It was too risky! Not enough stability for a family man. Unrealistic."

"I think you should have done it!"

"Well, maybe you're right." As the snowplow went by, the driver raised an apologetic hand to Dad, and Dad waved. "But, at the time, it seemed right not to. Everybody has to compromise their ideals, kiddo."

The snowplow turned the corner and I lowered my

voice. "Hey, Dad? How come you didn't want to run the orchard?"

Dad readjusted his stocking cap so that it covered his ears more completely. "It's not that I didn't want to run an orchard. It's just that I didn't want to run my father's."

"Why not?"

"Your grandpa was not exactly an easy person to get along with." Dad stuck his shovel into the snow and pushed his hands underneath his jacket. "I know how deeply you admire your grandpa. And rightly so! He was an honest, hard-working man. And he provided for his family the best way he knew how."

The edge of a shingle protruded from the bank of snow alongside the driveway. I pulled it out and pitched it toward the stack by the house. "So, what are you trying to say?"

"I guess . . . ah . . . I guess that he was a little too set in his ways. Very intolerant of change. Even if there was an easier, better way to do something, he wouldn't hear of it."

"Well, Dad," I cut in, "don't you think maybe he had to be that way? I mean, when your whole life depends on something like how much rain you get, don't you think you have to be single-minded about the way you do things?"

Dad's eyebrows are very bushy and he brushed off

the snow clinging to them. "To a degree," he said, "but I also think you have to be open to new ideas. Or at least respectful of the people who have them." Dad walked over to where I was standing. "Do you know that in the whole of my life Grandpa Warner never cared to hear my opinion on anything? He also never paid me a compliment, and it wasn't until he was on his deathbed that he could bring himself to say 'I love you.' Can you imagine how much those words would have meant to me before then?"

I tried to swallow, but my throat was frozen shut, my fists tightly clenched around the handle of the shovel.

Dad stared down at my hands. He suddenly smiled. "You're not going to hit me with that, are you?"

I loosened my grip. "No. . . . But I don't understand why you're telling me this."

"Grandpa Warner let his whole life go by without ever really getting involved. He knew as little as he had to about the world outside. He always wished things could be simpler. Like he imagined they were when he was a boy. And when he couldn't make that happen, he withdrew. Nobody could get through to him, and after a while, nobody tried. The truth is, when you don't need anybody, nobody needs you. It's as simple as that."

My body was rapidly heating. "I still don't see why

you're saying all this stuff! Why are you talking to me like this!" I turned away from him.

"Because in many ways you're a lot like Grandpa Warner." Dad grabbed my arms and turned me to face him. "Look, Caroline. I just don't want to picture you at the end of your life looking back with regret at the things you could have done and the people you could have loved. And Grandpa wouldn't have wanted that, either. You know that, don't you?"

I let the shovel fall with a bang. "So what you're saying is you want me to be someone else?"

"No, no, no. Not at all. I want you to be exactly who you are. And I want you to be aware of what's good and unique and to protect that. But when you get so guarded about yourself that nothing and no one has a place in your life, that's a pretty crummy waste."

The mailtruck swung into our driveway, and Dad went over to retrieve the mail.

"Let's go in and get warmed up," he said when he came back. He extended a hand to me. "Okay?"

I nodded numbly and followed him into the house. Mother was on the phone.

"Okay, Paul," she said into the receiver, "I'll try to make it in by seven. Thanks for calling. 'Bye."

"When did the phone get fixed?" Dad began sorting through the bundle of mail he'd brought in.

164

"Beats me," Mother answered. "I didn't even know it was working until Maddy called a little while ago. She wanted me to tell you, Caroline, that her party's been called off for tonight."

I unzipped my jacket. "Okay. Thanks."

"What'd Paul want?" Dad asked. Paul Lubbens is Mom's boss.

"He wants me to come in to work later on today. I guess a snowfall reminds people that Christmas is coming. He wants to try to open up around seven and thought he might be able to use me."

Dad extended a letter toward me. "Here's one for you!" he said, surprised.

"Who's it from?" Mom asked.

I took the letter and read the return address. "David Kettering," I mumbled.

"That name sounds familiar." Mom's forehead scrunched under the task of recollection.

I took my gloves off and shakily slid a thumbnail under the envelope flap. "I used to play with him in grade school."

"Oh, yes!" Mother's forehead relaxed. "I didn't even know he was still around! What does he want?"

"I don't know!" I said, annoyed. "Give me a chance!"

Both Mother and Dad turned away to think up something to do while I read my letter. It was written in longhand on notebook paper:

165

Dear Caroline,

Just wanted to drop you a line concerning the school newspaper. I hope you'll join us! Mr. Daverman showed me some of your poetry, and I know you'll be a real asset. Also, I think it would be fun getting to know each other again.

Please say you'll join the staff!

David

So. It had been David pushing for me. Not Maddy. When I finished reading the letter, Mother and Dad looked up expectantly but were not about to quiz me.

"David is the editor of our school paper," I explained, "and he wanted to invite me to be on the staff."

"That's wonderful!" Mother started to reach for the letter, then quickly drew her hand back.

"Are you going to do it?" Dad asked softly.

I folded the letter neatly and slipped it into the envelope. "I haven't really decided. I . . . I . . . probably . . ."

Dad sucked in his lower lip, slowly closing, then opening both eyes. "Would you like something hot to drink?"

"I . . . I don't really want anything. I think I'll just go to my room for a while." I didn't look back while making my exit. "Come on, Bill."

Old Bill plodded along at my side through the hall

to my room. As I soundlessly closed the door, he fell into an exhausted heap on the floor beside my bed. I sat on the edge of the bed, pulled off my socks, and wedged my feet underneath him. Old Bill was hardly breathing, he was so tired.

A small glass vase on my bedside table held the remains of the only marigold I'd picked all season. The water in the vase had evaporated away, leaving behind a greenish scum.

Last spring I'd chosen just the right seeds, painstakingly prepared the soil, planted the seeds with perfect spaces in between, protected them from insects and weeds and roadside litter, watered them and fertilized them. But it wasn't until I'd gone out to turn the soil over for winter that I realized I hadn't really enjoyed them.

So I'd picked one, and put it in water. But it had kind of been too late. It was only pretty for a day or two.

I tenderly lifted the rotted blossom from the vase and sat on the edge of my bed for a long time sadly clutching it. It was too late this year, but next year I could do things differently.

14

The walkway leading to Maddy's house had been shoveled bare, and the house number blared underneath the porch light. "One—seven—two—eight." Hmm. Two sets of two consecutive numbers: one and two, seven and eight. I hadn't noticed that before, but I guess that really should come as no surprise. I conveniently hadn't noticed a few other things.

Twenty-four hours ago I never would have believed I'd be standing outside Maddy's front door. But, there I was—shaking like a leaf—and grateful

Maddy was more tolerant of me than I would have been of her.

Mother had dropped me off on her way to work. Her last words to me as I got out of the car were, "Remember, now. Mr. Lindsay is Dad's new boss, so mind your manners."

I chuckled nervously to myself. What did she think I was going to do? Sit down at the table, point to something and shout, "Gimme some of that!"?

As it was, calling Maddy earlier in the day and accepting her invitation to have dinner with her family were two of the hardest things I've ever had to do.

My hand shook as I rang the bell. It was answered almost immediately by Tyler.

He looked up at me, said, "Go away!" and slammed the door shut. I stood there not knowing what to do. After a few moments I raised my hand to ring again, but the door was opened before I pushed the bell.

"Are you Caroline? Come in," said a man trying to restrain Tyler. Tyler wrestled loose, kicked him, and ran off.

"That's Tyler," he said. "Please excuse his behavior. He's been cooped up in the house all day. Sometimes I wish I had half his energy!" The man extended his hand and I took it.

"I'm Maddy's father."

"How do you do," I said. He gripped my hand

tightly and it made me feel uncomfortable. Like I couldn't get away.

"Your hands are shaking!" Mr. Lindsay said, releasing his grip. "You must be cold. Come in. I believe dinner is just about ready."

Mr. Lindsay led the way to the dining room. Maddy was setting a wicker basket on the table as we walked in.

"Caroline! Hi!" Maddy turned to her father. "Why didn't you tell me she was here?" she asked impatiently.

"Let me take your coat, Caroline." I slipped it off and handed it to him. "Caroline just now got here," he explained. "I really wasn't trying to keep any secrets."

Maddy moved swiftly around the table as Mr. Lindsay left briefly to hang my coat up. "Let's sit here together," she said warmly. "Thanks for coming. I was so surprised when you called me this afternoon."

I nodded my head, my own thoughts in a spin as I groped for something to say. "I . . . I was surprised, too. And I was surprised that you invited me over for dinner. After—after the way I've been treating you. I've been a real creep."

Maddy smiled her most charming smile. "Yes. You have."

"I—it really didn't have anything to do with you," I apologized.

170

"That's good." Maddy nudged me. "Anyway, you're worth a little grief once in a while."

Tyler raced into the room imitating a siren in a high-pitched whine. He ran around and around the table, tapping everyone as he passed. Finally he stopped, pushed his place setting aside and plunked himself on the tabletop. He turned so he could stare at me.

A woman entered the room carrying two glasses of wine. "Are you Caroline? Hi. I'm Mrs. Lindsay. I'm so glad you could make it through all this snow! That was some blizzard!"

"Yes. Yes, it was," I answered. "I'm glad, well, thank you for inviting me. For dinner, I mean."

"We love it when Maddy has her friends in." Mrs. Lindsay looked so young! Radiant. There was a slight puffiness around her eyes, but they were sparkly, and her hair was shiny-sleek. She set the two goblets on the table between her and Mr. Lindsay.

"Wouldn't you like to sit in a chair, Tyler?" she asked sweetly.

Tyler squeezed his eyes shut and shook his head.

"It would be much easier to eat if you did," she reasoned.

"Not hungry," he said. When he opened his eyes they flashed.

"Well." Mrs. Lindsay paused. "You certainly don't have to eat if you're not hungry."

171

Having settled that, Tyler turned back to resume staring at me. I avoided his gaze.

Josie had been silently serving dinner. It was kind of weird. At home we just put everything on the table, and you can pick whatever you want. I studied the plate in front of me.

Mr. Lindsay cleared his throat. "You like pork chops, don't you, Caroline?"

"Yes, sir," I replied softly.

"It comes from a pig, you know. Oink! Oink! Oink!" Tyler screeched.

"That's right, Tyler," Mrs. Lindsay said. He stuck his tongue out at her.

Everyone began eating. Well, except for Tyler. He continued to glare at me, and I continued to ignore him.

"So, Caroline," Mr. Lindsay said. "Tell us a little about yourself."

A mandarin orange stuck halfway down my throat.

"Daddy!" Maddy protested.

"Well, I mean about your family. I've met your father, as I'm sure you know."

"Yes. He's really looking forward to Monday," I said weakly.

"Believe me," Mr. Lindsay said, "we're really looking forward to Monday, too. We all feel so fortunate to have found someone with your dad's qualifications living right here in town. He is direly needed!" Mr.

Lindsay stabbed at his salad with a fork. "So, tell me, do you have any brothers or sisters?"

I took a sip of water. "No, ah . . . no. I only have a dog. Well," I stammered, "he's not really mine. I mean he doesn't live with us or anything. Well, he lives with my grandma. Right next door. Well, ah, no. Just plain no. I don't have any brothers or sisters."

"Does your mother work?" Mr. Lindsay continued. He looked amused.

"Yes. She works at Klugg's. That's a department store. She's a buyer."

"That's where I got this sweater!" Mrs. Lindsay smoothed her cuffs.

"It's really pretty," I said.

She smiled. "Thank you."

I cut a piece of asparagus and put it in my mouth.

"You're going to get green pee," Tyler commented.

I shrugged my shoulders but didn't look at him.

"Has she worked there long?"

"Well, ah, no. The store was just built not too long ago." It was hard to talk or do anything with Tyler staring at me. "And she didn't want to work before that. She thought it was important to stay home with me when I was young. Ah, younger."

"Well, I applaud her," Mr. Lindsay said, placing a hand on Mrs. Lindsay's shoulder.

Mrs. Lindsay stiffened slightly and moved away from his touch. "So. Have you lived here long?"

"What is this?" Maddy asked. "Twenty questions?"

"Oh, I'm sorry," Mrs. Lindsay said apologetically. She pushed her plate aside and lit a cigarette. "I certainly didn't mean to pry."

I could still sense Tyler staring at me. Finally, I decided staring back might do the trick.

When our eyes met, Tyler sprang into action. "You're ugly!" he shouted. "I don't like you!" He jumped down from his perch on the table and ran from the room.

Mrs. Lindsay chased after him. "Tyler! You come back here right now and apologize!"

Maddy threw her napkin on the floor. "You oughta belt that little brat!"

"Nobody's going to hit anybody," Mr. Lindsay said calmly. He turned to me. "I apologize for Tyler. He's a little spoiled."

"A little!" Maddy gasped.

Mr. Lindsay ignored her. "He didn't mean what he said. He was just testing us. Please just try to overlook his comment. There certainly is no truth to it." Mr. Lindsay and Maddy have the same smile.

I picked at the food on my plate, not knowing what to say.

"Come on, Caroline," Maddy said, her voice strained. "Let's go to my room."

Josie appeared in the doorway. "Telephone call for you, Caroline."

"She'll take it in my room," Maddy decided.

174

"Thank you for dinner," I said as I rose from the table. "It was very good."

"You are very welcome," Mr. Lindsay said. "I think Josie's got something for dessert if you girls get hungry later."

I followed behind Maddy as we scurried up the stairs. Maddy pointed in the direction of her phone. I raced to pick it up.

"Hello?"

"Hi, Sweetie. It's Mother. How's it going?"

"Fine." My answer was interrupted by a click as someone replaced the receiver on the kitchen phone.

"The reason I'm calling," Mother said, "is because I'm going to be leaving here in about a half hour. The store is pretty dead, and I'm not really needed here tonight. I guess there aren't as many adventurous souls out there as we thought! So, anyway, I wondered if I should swing by and pick you up on my way home."

"Okay. Well, just a minute."

I placed my hand over the receiver. "My mother wants to pick me up in a half hour."

Disappointment creased Maddy's face for just a moment, then quickly disappeared. "Why don't you spend the night here?"

"I don't have any of my stuff with me. And, besides, don't you have to ask your parents first?"

"Nah. They won't mind. You can wear one of my

175

nightgowns, and I'm sure we have an extra toothbrush around here somewhere."

"Are you sure it's okay?"

"Positive."

"Mother?" I said into the phone. "Would it be all right if I spent the night at Maddy's?"

There was a slight pause. "Well, yes . . . I guess that'd be all right. That'd be fine! What time should I pick you up tomorrow?"

"Oh, I don't know. We'll figure something out and I'll call you in the morning."

"Okay! I guess I'll see you whenever, then," Mother agreed. She sounded pretty pleased. "Bye-bye!"

" 'Bye."

After I'd hung up the phone, I turned toward Maddy. She was sitting on the edge of the bed. For just an instant I could see in her the little girl she used to be.

"What's wrong, Maddy?"

"Sorry about tonight. You know. About what happened at dinner. I wanted it to be special. I wish Laura could have been here. I wish things could have been the way they used to be."

"It's okay," I assured her. "The dinner was special. And I think your family is really nice. Josie, too."

Maddy pressed the center of an air bubble in her comforter. "Well, they're not."

176

I sat down next to Maddy on the edge of the bed. "Maddy! How can you stand to say things like that about your own family?"

Maddy clasped her hands and bent her fingers back. Some of her knuckles cracked. "Because it's true. I told you how they treated Laura and me."

"But they didn't do anything on purpose! I just don't believe that! You know what I think?"

"What is it, O Great And Wise One?" Maddy gave a sarcastic bow.

"I think it's ugly when you go around blaming people when things don't go right."

Maddy's knuckles were white. I'd begun to think maybe I'd better catch Mother before she left the store when Maddy leaned over and pulled a small cardboard box from a drawer in her bedside table.

The box was jammed with snapshots, letters, notes, dried flowers, matchbooks, and scores of other mementos. Maddy searched through it and found a stack of pictures secured with a rubber band. She slipped the rubber band over her wrist. "I found some pictures I want to show you."

Maddy sorted through her fistful of photographs, then handed one to me. "Here's a picture of Laura and me on my first birthday. Laura was three then."

The two little girls were standing on chairs by the dining room table. There was a gaily decorated cake in front of them with a candle in its center. Maddy was holding her hands up with glee and sporting a huge, two-toothed grin. Laura's face was placid. She had the stunned look of an angel who'd accidentally fallen to earth. Misplaced.

"Isn't Laura gorgeous?" Maddy whispered.

I nodded my head in agreement.

Maddy handed me another picture. "Here's one of us with my mom."

In this picture, the girls were a bit older. "Maddy! You look exactly like your mother!" Laura had her back to the camera and was holding a sprig of lilac.

"Yeah, I know," Maddy said. "It's kind of spooky. Here. Look at this one. This is what my mom looked like in college."

The young woman in the photograph had long, flowing hair pinned back on each side with a flower. She was wearing patched bell-bottomed jeans and a floppy gauze shirt unbuttoned one button too far. The group of people around her were dressed pretty much the same, and most were holding signs. The only word I could make out on the sign Maddy's mother was holding was "LIFE." "What was she doing?" I asked.

"Protesting something. The Vietnam War, probably." Maddy took the picture from me and fondled it. "I found this in Laura's room after she went away. Laura was really into the sixties' culture. I don't know.

178

It was like she was trying to relive the things that were important to my mother. Oh, look!" Maddy held out another photo. "My dad's in this one. Look how long his hair was!" She laughed. "What a riot!"

"Well, except for that," I said, "he doesn't really look that much different."

"He is." Maddy snatched the picture from me and tossed it back into the box. "He's changed a lot."

"Like how?" I hardly dared ask the question. The veins in Maddy's neck were throbbing.

"He only cares about what he's going to be doing each day. Know what I mean?"

"No."

"Well, it's like he doesn't care about big things anymore. He used to. He and my mother were always rallying for or against something. He used to have ideals. You know. About politics and things like that. Now he just concentrates on his own life. I don't know. I can't really explain it. It's like he made a compromise, or something." Maddy smoothed her hair. "If I ever find any causes to be passionate about, I'm going to stay passionate forever," she vowed. "I just have such a longing in me to care about things."

I smiled at her. "Hey, Maddy? What do you think happened to Laura? I know her mother died, but she was your mother, too, and you're okay. . . ."

Maddy twirled the rubber band on her wrist. "How

can you ever know what goes on inside another person? Anyway, Laura won't talk to me. I've really tried, too." Maddy stretched the rubber band to its limit and let it snap back against her skin. I got a bitter taste in my mouth.

"I've thought about it a lot, though," Maddy continued softly. "And I think I have at least an idea." Maddy bent over and lifted a music box from the cardboard container at her feet. "Isn't this pretty? My parents got it when they lived in Germany."

I shook my head.

"A few weeks after Laura left I went through her belongings and found a lot of clues." Maddy slid off the bed and sat on the floor beside me.

"Laura had a ton of books. She had a lot of biographies on people who were popular in the sixties and died young. Everybody from the Kennedys and Martin Luther King to Jimi Hendrix and Janis Joplin. Jim Morrison. A few others."

"The last people you mentioned are the ones on all the posters, aren't they?"

Maddy nodded. "Laura had a lot of their records. Well, most of them belonged to my mother. The other books she had were pretty weird. Books on things like witchcraft and the occult, satanism, reincarnation, Eastern religions. Time travel. I also found two notebooks. One was filled with charts and graphs, and the other with Laura's poetry."

180

"Could I read some of it?"

"I don't have it anymore. The poems were so awful. Violent. All about things like sacrificing the lamb and traveling through the darkness to find the light and when would be the best time to die so that her plane would cross my mother's. I didn't really understand any of it. I think that's what all the charts were about."

I couldn't stop the shudder that passed through me.

"That's the way I felt," Maddy said, noticing my unease. "And that's why I burned everything. All of it. The charts and books and records and all the poems. Well, except for one." Maddy opened the music box and drew out a faded and yellowed piece of paper. "I don't know why I kept it, really."

The creases in the paper were nearly worn through— as though it had been folded and unfolded a thousand times or so. Scrawled across the page were these words:

> Somewhere on an island so far away
> you can scarcely imagine it
>
> There lives the child who was me
> and when I am so cold
>
> I can call upon her to take it all
> away and make it all okay

"Oh, Maddy." I drew my knees up to rest my head on them.

"She's better. Laura is." Maddy put her hand on my back.

"Do you ever get to see her?"

"Not often. Not at all for the past year. But I write to her at least once a week. About everything." Maddy smiled at me lovingly. "I've told her all about you. And I've even sent her copies of some of your poems. I—I hope that's okay."

"That's fine," I said. "But, ah, what did you tell her about me?"

Maddy chuckled. "Fishing for compliments?"

"Sort of. At least I hope so."

"Well . . ." Maddy's gaze was so intense my cheeks burned. "I told her that after Mother died I went just about as far out of myself as she went into herself. But that now I have a friend who's making me want to find my way back."

All five hundred pounds of me just sat there like a stump. "I've been such a jerk."

"See? I told you we had a lot in common," Maddy teased. "And, you know what? About a week ago I got a postcard from Laura! It's the first time in almost three years that she's contacted me. I want to show it to you." Maddy took the postcard from her music box and handed it to me.

The front of the card pictured a simple sketch of a butterfly, and neatly handwritten on the back was:

Maddy—

> the walls here get
> clearer every
>> TIME
> I blinkblink at them
> they have given me the
>> BEST MEDICINE
> I hold my sides the
> laughter comes so
>> HARD
>>> —Laura—

I turned the postcard over and over in my hands, not knowing what to say. The poem didn't seem to be written by a well person.

"I know, I know," Maddy said, interpreting my silence. "The poem is still sad. But if feeling pain is a sign of life, then at least she's showing a sign of life." Maddy pulled at the rubber band around her wrist. It slipped off and snapped me in the hand.

"Ouch!" I yelped. "What are you trying to do?" I asked, rubbing the welt on my hand. "See if I can feel pain?"

"Uh-huh!" Maddy laughed. "And, congratulations! You passed the test!"

"Well, Maddy." I sighed. "Whatever will become of us?"

"I don't know. Sometimes I wonder if we'll ever be eighty years old and have an album of perfect memories."

"Yeah," I agreed. "It could be that we'll have an atom bomb dropped on us tomorrow, and that'd be the end of everything."

"Nah," Maddy said. "I don't think we're that lucky."

"Maddy!" I nudged her leg. "What a terrible thing to say! Horrible!"

Maddy looped her arm through mine. "Wouldn't it be neat if we could take the good things about ourselves and melt them together, then each take half? We'd be two outstanding people. We'd be awesome."

"Or else," I suggested, "we could just be the kind of friends who yell at each other a lot."

Maddy rolled her eyes. "Ooh! That sounds like fun! You have *such* a way with words, Caroline."

"Yeah. Now if I could only train them to come out of my mouth as well as my pen . . ."

"I love just about everything that comes out of your mouth," Maddy said affectionately.

I shrugged my shoulders. "I don't know. Sometimes I feel like a giant zit on the face of mankind."

"Oh! That's great!" Maddy whooped. "By the way," she teased, "I loved it when you told my dad you didn't have any brothers or sisters, but you almost had a dog." She laughed.

184

I covered my face with my hands. "I am so embarrassed."

Maddy let go of my arm and moved a few inches away. "Speaking of pets, did I ever tell you about the cat I used to have?"

"No, but I bet I'm going to hear it," I answered dryly.

Maddy ignored me and plunged into her story. "Well, it was shortly after my mother died. One of our neighbor's cats had kittens, and they gave one to Laura and me. It was gray. Really cute. We named him Ashes."

"How original."

Maddy nudged me. "We were young! What do you expect?"

I settled back against the bed.

"So, anyway, Laura and I just loved that kitten. We were pushing it around in a doll buggy one day, and this kid who lived near us stopped to look at it. And you know what he said?"

"I can't imagine." I smiled.

Maddy blinked her eyes. "He said that cats inherit the souls of dead people. Wasn't that a horrible thing to say? Especially to us?"

I pulled a face. "Uh-huh."

"We thought my mother's soul was inside the cat." Maddy put her hand on her throat. "We were so freaked out! The cat used to perch on our bed at night and stare at us." Maddy laughed. "He probably thought we were a couple of real space cadets, but we thought it was Mother watching us. Anyway"—Maddy looked a little teary—"Laura and I prayed that the cat would run away, and he did! I still feel guilty about that. I wonder if Laura does, too."

"Oh, Maddy! You don't really think you willed your mother away, do you? Or the cat?"

"No. Not really. I'm sure it was just a coincidence that the cat ran away. Anyway, I still have a lot of times when I'm sure I can feel my mother's presence."

I reached over to touch Maddy's arm and the warmth of Grandpa Warner's sunshiny cove passed straight through me. It took my breath away.

"I know what you mean."

Oh, Grandpa. I have looked for you in all the wrong places.